SLAUGHTER ON THE SCENE...

Ben Slaughter unlocked the door, took a step inside and stopped. The hotel room was a shambles. The nightstand and chair were shattered. The bedstead looked as if it had been struck with a sledge hammer. The mattress was half onto the floor; it was drenched with blood.

Frank Littlejohn lay on the floor under the window, his throat cut. His pale gray eyes stared sightlessly at the ceiling. His clothing was partially ripped from his body. One boot was off. Blood streaked the grime-encrusted window above him. Ben swallowed hard; he took a deep breath and moved into the room. He closed the door, causing a loud clattering noise. He turned and saw that a hatchet had been stuck in the door and had fallen when he closed it.

Whoever had done this, Ben knew, had not found what they were looking for—the deadly prize they called ''The Dragon's Eye.''

Novels by
E. B. Majors

Slaughter and Son #1
Slaughter and Son #2: Nightmare Trail

Published by
WARNER BOOKS

SLAUGHTER

& SON ②

NIGHTMARE TRAIL

E. B. MAJORS

WARNER BOOKS

A Warner Communications Company

One

The new Baldwin ten-wheeler chased its yellow eye into the oncoming night. Bert Slaughter sat one car forward the mail car eyeing the dimming landscape sweeping past. St. Louis was five hours behind them. Missouri was giving out, the border and Kansas City coming up. Bert did not talk to the man beside him. Could not. He was a Belgian. The only English he knew was "yesssss," said with a vigorous nod of his shining head. Bert did not speak his language, Walloon. Didn't want to. Why, he'd wondered aloud to son Ben earlier, didn't the whole world speak English? Why did there have to be six or seven hundred different lingoes nobody savvied, except the people who used them? It just made for confusion, arguments, wars, and suchlike. Even little tads could speak English. How come two grown men couldn't? He blamed their parents.

He got out half a plug of Battle Ax tobacco; he bit off a chunk and politely offered the man a chaw. The Belgian twitched his nose and waved it away. You'd think it was poison, thought Bert.

They were not seated together by chance; they were assigned to the same job. In the safe in the mail car behind them was a collection of diamonds, rubies, emeralds, and other jewels, beauties all. Bigger and shinier than Bert had ever seen. The Belgian crown jewels had been on public display in New

York, Chicago, and St. Louis. San Francisco was next; then they'd be returned to Antwerp.

They *were* something to see alright, admitted Bert to himself. If gewgaws tickled your fancy. And worth about $2 million. Their value was beyond price to King Leopold II and the royal family, so his son and partner Ben said. And to the U.S. government, honored by the loan of them. Thanks to the New York office's dickering, the government had contracted with Wells Fargo to protect them during their visit. James B. Hume, Wells Fargo's chief of detectives, had assigned Detectives Bert and Ben Slaughter the job. The Belgians had sent over two secret service men to double the protection. Which was why Bert came to be seated beside the middle-aged, pink, little man who didn't like Battle Ax, while Ben shared duty in the mail car with the man's partner.

"Kansas City coming up!" boomed the conductor. "Ten minutes." He stood at the far end of the car swaying. "All passengers collect your things for getting off. All through-passengers, we will be stopped for twelve minutes. If you get off, board the train soon as you hear the whistle."

"Ginzess Zeddi?" asked the Belgian.

"Huh?"

"Ginzess . . ."

The conductor was passing. "Kansas City, right. You getting off?"

"No," said Bert. "What time you got?"

"Seven fifty-two." The conductor went on. Bert slumped in his seat; he tilted his Stetson over his eyes. "Eight minutes to changeover, relax."

"Relics?"

Bert groaned. Eyes closed, he pictured Ben on a crate in the mail car talking to the man's partner. Both spoke French, as did this one. The three of them jabbered away when they first met. Bert felt left out, but pride glowed inside him. Ben was a graduate of the University of Virginia. He had mastered more than French in his four years in Charlottesville; he'd graduated *summa cum laude*. With his background, why he had gone to work for Wells Fargo, why he tore about after trash on the hoof, courted trouble and dodged lead, all for eighty a month plus expenses, was more than Bert could savvy. They argued and argued about it, but there seemed no way he could get him to quit, and find something better suited to his fine mind and expensive education.

This job was a good example: mother-henning a hatful of colored stones, traipsing about the country with them. What a bore. They didn't have five minutes to themselves. The Belgians refused to switch partners, so each was stuck with one. And the train rolled on. Three days on the fastest train through the world's greatest scenery was more than Bert could abide; this trip was thirty-eight. They'd be zig-zagging across the plains, crawling over the Rockies and Sierra; the food was wretched, no booze, sleep was on a seat hard as a tombstone. What upset him more than anything was Ben's attitude. He liked working with the foreigners, liked talking French, liked helping his partner with his English.

Liked it all because his father hated it, that's why! Bert grunted and curled his lip. He liked and admired his son, but he did have a traitorous streak. He purely loved to rub his father the wrong way.

Bert pushed his hat up and side-eyed the Belgian. He stared blankly straight ahead; he sucked his mustache, he drummed his fat fingers against his knees. He'd sat so and drummed so since Pennsylvania Station in New York. Bert sniffed. He didn't even know where Belgium was. He glanced out the window and wished *something* would happen to break the monotony. Not a train wreck, maybe just a squabble among the four card players at the other end of the car. Maybe a tornado, a small one. A holdup? *Some* kind of action!

He carried no watch; the position of the sun by day and the stars by night told him the time. Close enough. He figured it to be eight. Time to change the guard. Four on, four off. He stood up, stretched, the train jolted, down he sat. He elbowed the Belgian.

"Time to . . ." He tapped the front of his waist where there was no watch pocket. "Time, time."

"Yesssssss."

They picked their way down the aisle. They passed the

necessary to the vestibule. The door to the mail car beckoned. Ben inside returned Bert's wave. The door was unlocked for them. The other Belgian nodded to Bert. He began jabbering to his friend. The changeover routine began: the clerk unlocked the Cincinnati Safe, the large, square, leather carrying case was brought out, and one by one the six drawers pulled. The jewels glittered. Bert sucked in his breath. Beautiful. Back into the safe went the case and the door was relocked. To Bert it was ridiculous, a waste of eyesight and time. Unnecessary.

One of the jewels stuck to the screen of his imagination: the large, blood-red ruby centerstone of King Leopold's crown. It was called the Dragon's Eye and was the favorite bauble of every Belgian king since Belgian kings began when the country separated fron Holland. Bert knew nothing about Belgium's history and cared less. But when the Dragon's Eye caught his, he was impressed. All the other jewels seemed to fade into gray. What a beauty...

"Stay awake," said Ben.

Bert ignored him. Kansas City arrived. Through the locked side door they could hear the activity on the station platform. Bert checked his Peacemaker. The Belgian eyed him. He carried a .32 with a mother-of-pearl grip. Bert wondered what kind of power something so little and light could possibly have. He would bet it couldn't dent a chicken. How good the man was with it was another question. He sure didn't look the secret service type; Bert pictured him perched on a stool, pen in hand, adding up figures. He wondered if he closed his eyes when he fired; wondered if he two-handed the gun the way Ben did when he'd started out.

Kansas City slipped behind them. It took the crowd, the bright lights, the tall buildings. The twin rails headed out across the darkened sunshine state. Bert sat on Ben's crate, legs dangling. He chewed; he enjoyed; he sent a brown strool into the nearest corner. The mail clerk was busy pigeon-holing letters from two sacks picked up in Kansas City; he stopped and eyed Bert over his spectacles.

"You just spit on government property."

"I spit in the corner."

"This is a U.S. mail car."

"So?"

"Government property."

"Government property should have a garboon."

He opened a cabinet under his worktable. He set a brass spittoon in the corner.

"Thanks."

Bert chewed; he let fly. And missed by four inches. The clerk threw up his hands. On rolled the train. Two days to Denver, two more to Salt Lake City, two more, maybe three across the flat, up the Sierra, down into the San Joaquin Valley to the City by the Bay. San Francisco could not come fast enough. Although with it would come a meeting with James B. Hume, Superintendant John Valentine, and President Lloyd Tevis. To him, Tevis was a wolf in snake's clothing. He had stolen Wells Fargo and Company from Henry Wells and Bill Fargo eleven years back. Ben kept saying stolen was too strong a word. It wasn't strong enough for him. A wolf in snake's clothing. Anybody who stole another fellow's business was. Still, if Hume could stand working for Tevis, he guessed he could. Of course he didn't much like working for Hume. Mr. Stiffneck, Sermon-mouth. Didn't like his stinking greaser cigars, his picking and needling.

Oh well, he wouldn't have to see any of them till after the exhibition. He got up from the crate.

"I'm goin' up ahead an' see what's goin' on with the boys."

The clerk glared. "You're not supposed to set foot out of this car. Not till midnight." He glanced at the Belgian. "He's on duty."

"Yessssss."

"You'd prob'ly snitch if I ducked out to take a leak."

"You'll have to wait till one minute after twelve."

"I bet in school you was the class snitch."

The clerk flushed; he tightened his jaw; he was about to respond when two shots rang in quick succession; the wood around the end doorlock splintered. The assembly caved in, smashed by a boot.

"Get 'em up!" said a cleanshaven man. He looked like a choir director.

Bert, the Belgian, and the clerk raised their hands. In he came; two others followed. Bert and the Belgian were disarmed, their weapons tossed into the spittoon corner. The trembling, white-faced clerk was pushed against the wall.

"Open her up, quick!"

"It's time locked . . ."

The blast filled the car. It slammed Bert's eardrums hard against his brain. Smoke curled from the gun muzzle. The clerk slumped to the floor; his hands framed a crimson flower at his chest.

"Jeez . . ." Bert gaped.

The killer swung on him. "Now you know we mean business!"

The train slowed. Bert's mind raced. Slick. They didn't stop the train to hold it up; they boarded in Kansas City with other passengers.

"OPEN IT!" shouted the killer at the Belgian. He stared.

"Sure," said Bert, "jus' give us the combination."

"We don't . . ."

"You jus' shot the only one who does."

"Nice goin', Jethro," said the choir director.

"Shut up callin' me by name, Orland Bisby!"

"Cross my heart, Jethro," said Bert. "We dunno. This boy here's from 'cross the pond. He can't even read American numbers."

"Never mind," said the third man. "Open the side door."

A small herd of horses was outside. Two men minded them. Bert's and the Belgian's guns were tossed out into the darkness. The third man stuck a blob of blasting gelatin to the door. He pushed a fuse in and lit it.

Bert jammed his fingers into his ears as it blew. The stink of cordite filled the air. He coughed. The blast blew the safe door clear. The jewel container inside was only tilted to one side. Jethro snatched it up. Away the three galloped while the two minders hurried the rest of the horses up the train. Men came flying out of the cars, mounted up, and rode off.

Bert and the Belgian were down in the ditch. They found their guns. Ben and the other man ran up. The passengers carried on loudly; two women shrilled. The brakeman ran up and down the train. The engineer was wounded; the fireman helped him down from his cab.

"They're heading west for Reno," said Ben. "The brakeman says there's a farm about two hundred yards east of here. Let's get some horses."

Bert sniffed. "Why waste your time? We don't stand a friggin' chance o' catchin' up with 'em."

• • • •

It took barely six minutes to get mounted and onto the trail. Bert was still sour on the chase.

"They could cut north or south, double back; they'd be dumb as goats to keep on to Reno."

"We'll soon see," said Ben. He bent low over his mare alongside his father.

"What a stinkin' dirty trick!"

"What?"

"Gettin' on at the station, 'steada' bushwackin' us out in the countryside. Shootin' folks in col' blood, no neckerchiefs over their faces, didn' even take the time to clean out the passengers. Rank amateurs. It's disgustin' . . ."

"We'll catch up to them by Reno."

"Sure. Look at your two friends; scared outta' their galluses we'll wind up shootin' it out."

Ben urged his horse forward; he moved a length, then two, ahead out of earshot. The two Belgians *did* look concerned, as well they might. The clerk's death was another thing, but Bert's rundown on all the black aspects wasn't what he wanted to hear. Better hooves ahead.

His father doted on pessimism; it fed something in him, without it he'd probably crawl under his shadow, curl up, and die. But he sure could be depressing!

The night flew by; it took the moon and rushed away the stars. The hot breeze whined. Lonely willows stood along the banks of the creek on their right. Reno's lights loomed. They drew closer; the town looked to be buttoned up for the night. A yellow light swathed the main street. It came from the saloon door and the windows at either side of it. Horses lined both sides of the street. Ben pointed to a tight group hitched two doors up from the saloon. The horses' flanks gleamed. The only ones they could see that were sweating.

"What a break," said Ben.

"Don't go countin' your chickens. They could just as easy belong to some what come in from the other end; ranch hands in town for a drunk, the local grange, drovers passin' through . . ."

"It's them. You're just disappointed because we caught up."

"They still got us twelve or fourteen to four . . ."

"We'll get help."

"No, sir. They jerked us aroun', we return the favor. Them are the rules. We got surprise on our side. They're inside settin' fire to their guts, celebratin' to beat the band, never dreamin' the fist o' God is 'bout to come down an' hammer 'em straight to hell."

"Let's find the marshal."

"No! Will you just once listen to your old man?"

Ben sighed. Bert took over. They loosed the outlaws' horses and led them down an alley to behind the saloon. They went back, crossed the street, and stood opposite the batwing doors.

"Take your friend an' go down the way," said Bert. "Cross over down past where their horses were."

Ben started off with his partner.

"Don' open up till we do. We'll trap 'em in a crossfire. They'll never know what hit 'em."

"You hope."

Ben and the other kept to the storefront shadows. Bert checked his iron. The little Belgian did likewise. Patrons came and went, the batwing doors rarely still. The clamor inside continued. Nearly an hour crawled by.

"We should go in an' haul 'em out," said Bert.

"Yessssss."

"No! Be patient. They'll show."

Twenty minutes later out they came. The unnamed third man in the mail car was followed by Jethro. He carried the collection case in plain sight. Orland and the others trooped out after them. The ones in the lead were the first to notice their horses were gone. They pulled up; they went for their guns. Bert and the Belgian stepped forward.

"GET 'EM UP!"

Bert fired inches over Jethro's hat. Ben's gun sounded in echo. Bert's order froze the outlaws. Some had half-raised their hands. The lot burst into action, a human pinwheel. They rushed forth dodging lead; they hurled themselves into alleys, behind horse troughs, a parked Washoe wagon, any cover. Reno filled with gunfire. The detectives' four-second edge paid off; the Slaughters and the Belgians cut down five of them. Bert emptied his gun. He fumbled the cylinder full and got off three more shots. He pitched one man into view from behind the right corner of the saloon. The man screamed, clutched his chest, and dropped on his face. A second man at the same corner reached out to pull him back. Bert's fourth shot found meat just under his shoulder; he tumbled over his friend's body. People crowded the doors of the saloon; they wide-eyed the action, but none came out to join it.

The detectives needed no help. The crossfire was murderous. The outlaws could find no real protection from it. Lead flew at them from two directions. A massacre.

"WE GIVE UP! WE GIVE UP!" yelled Jethro. "You want 'em, you got 'em. Don't shoot no more!"

He came out from behind the Washoe wagon. He waved one gloved hand and set the case down. Up went his hands. It was all over. Five were dead, four wounded; four gave up. The Belgians collected the survivors. Ben counted dead and living. He frowned. Bert spoke Ben's mind.

"Two missin'." He glared at Jethro. "Where are they?"

"What two?" Orland asked.

"Don' try to diddle me, goatface; there was fifteen o' you, three in the mail car, ten with the passengers an' up front holdin' the crew, two mindin' your horses. I counted the horses."

"They took off," said Jethro.

Ben holstered his gun. "I'll get after them."

"The devil take 'em," said his father.

The two Belgians examined the contents of the case. One pulled open the bottom drawer.

"*Sacré merde!*" The other groaned. Both stared at Bert.

King Leopold's crown. In all its glory. Almost all. The centerstone was missing. The Dragon's Eye.

Two

Chief James B. Hume stood at one of the two windows of his office overlooking San Francisco Bay. He tugged at his La Flor de Portuondo, Chicos cigar. His handsome face was shadowed with concern.

"It was Temple Riverton's idea to volunteer the company as watchdogs. The New York office called the turn and we have to dance to it."

"It's not our usual cup of tea, I admit," said John J. Valentine. He was superintendent of operations; he was wapper-jawed, chesty. His eyes at the moment were fixed in a flinty stare at Hume's broad back. The chief faced him.

"It's a job for the Pinkertons, not us. I told Riverton, but he'd already sounded out Mr. Tevis. Sold him on the publici-ty angle. Insists guarding valuables in transit is all in a day's work for Wells Fargo. Idiot! By the Lord Harry, we can thank our stars nothing's gone wrong. They should be here Friday. Cross your fingers they'll get here intact."

"How long will they be on display?"

"All next week. At the museum. Haven't you seen the posters? They're plastered all over town."

"What happens after the exhibition?"

"They're off to Australia. Out of our hands, thank God."

"Relax, James; if anything does happen, Riverton'll be the one Tevis'll come down on, not you."

"That's not the point. This thing's a powder keg. If

anything does happen, it could turn into an international incident. Telegrams back and forth between Washington and Antwerp, ambassadors huddling, the president jumping in looking for heads to lop off. You know old Unconditional Surrender, he'd raise the roof. The company'd be on the pan and cooking with the flame high.

"John, I never want another contract like this ever again! Guarding valuables in transit is one thing; responsibility for their safekeeping while on display, no thank you. The rule book clearly specifies the nature and limitations of the company's services. I wish Mr. Tevis'd look at it once in awhile."

"It's Henry Wells' and Bill Fargo's brainchild; Tevis didn't write it; he pays no attention to it. All he cares about is the color of our ink. Now for pity's sakes, will you stop worrying? You'll fret yourself into an ulcer."

"I could wring Riverton's neck!"

"Nothing's happened, nothing's going to."

Hume glared. He wanted to argue; dearly wished to to occupy his mind and mouth with something other than the gnawing problem at hand. Before he could get a word out, the door rattled under female knuckles. His secretary, blonde and pretty Albertina Preble, stuck her head in.

"Telegram, Mr. Hume."

"Who from?"

"Mr. Slaughter. The young one."

Hume flew across the room. He snatched the wire from her. He realized he was being rude as he did and smiled thinly in apology; he tore open the envelope with trembling hands.

"Take it easy," said Valentine.

"Ohhhhhhh myyyyyyyy Godddddddd. . . ."

• • • •

July in Kansas. The heavens locked their cisterns, the Plains blazed with heat. Once in awhile a light shower escaped the clouds and dashed upon the ground, only to run for cover into the creek and river beds and leave the roots of all growing things as thirsty as ever. A little rain was worse than none. After a brief splattering, the sun would come out and bake the earth as hard as brick.

Kansas was not farming country; so said Bert Slaughter. Much too dry. Cattle country maybe. Blizzard for sure. Most of all just plain dry.

Along the streams the corn looked like patches of sticks. Sorry-looking vegetable gardens shriveled; most of the wells and springs gave out early; water in creeks lay so shallow it didn't have the strength to flow. It sat in a succession of puddles. Now and again the southwest wind blew out of the ovens of the western deserts. It swept the land with a flinty dust. The old joke was repeated: "Got to soak the pigs at night so's they can hold their swill."

The nights were as rough as the days. Rougher. Night was supposed to offer relief from the heat. It didn't. Not in Kansas. Not in July.

Bert had tracked the two thieves with the Dragon's Eye for two nights and two days. The only animal on earth tireder than he was his horse. It was a fit and willing little mare, willing to a point. He could feel with his thighs that her heart wasn't in it any longer. She obeyed his heels; his soothing words made her. Even while his own heart was losing interest.

His thoughts went back to Ben, the two Belgians, and the prisoners. They would be locked up in Reno overnight. In the morning they'd be run back to Kansas City to stand trial. The Belgians would contact their ambassador in Washington with the good news. When word that the Eye had been stolen reached the embassy, it would be flashed home to Belgium. There'd be a complaint; Wells Fargo would be called on the carpet; from the Secret Service on down to the marshal of every one-hitch-rack town in the territories, everybody would be alerted; a reward would be posted.

"Whatta mess o' slops . . ."

He wiped the dust from his face for the hundredth time. He narrowed his eyes and peered into the moonlit landscape ahead. He had pushed the mare for nearly half an hour in hopes of catching up. To at least within sight of the two. All he asked for at this stage was a glimpse of their horses and their hats so he could indentify them if and when they stopped.

Gypsum. So said Orland Bisby, the choir director. He'd pressed the pale little man for their destination just before he'd mounted up. He'd barked at him; it scared him into answering truthfully, he hoped.

Gypsum could be a lie. Along about now Orland could be laughing up his sleeve. He'd know soon. It couldn't be more than four miles ahead, if he could rely on the signpost two miles back.

"Jeez. . . ."

It suddenly struck him. The Belgians would contact their people; would Ben contact James Hume in San Francisco? He couldn't be that lily-livered; rash; stupid . . . But he couldn't very well hold it back. If the company got word of it from the Belgians, even worse from Washington, there'd be the devil to pay!

Ben'd *have* to spill the rotten beans. And *he* would have to catch up with them, get back the ruby, head straight for Frisco. With a little luck he could be there before the rest of the collection. Was that where the rest were heading? Must be. Ben and the Belgians wouldn't lock them up in some podunk bank to wait out the storm. That'd only mess things up even worse.

"Jeez. . . ."

Boy, would the newspapers have a field day with this one! They'd roast Wells Fargo to a cinder. Lloyd Tevis would roast James Hume, Hume would roast him, he'd roast Ben. Oh heck, he couldn't do that. The fault had to be sliced up equally among the four of them.

On he rode. He rounded a rutted curve; he came within sight of Gypsum.

"Orland, you'd by God better be tellin' the truth. If you lied by God I'll hang you with your own longjohns; so help me!"

Three

Gypsum was bigger than Reno. It had two saloons: the Gypsum Palace and Ogilvy's Saloon and Restaurant—Ladies Invited. Bert hit it lucky. He arrived just in time to catch sight of two men ambling into the Palace. The dust caking their horses was streaked with sweat. From what he could see, they had stopped to talk before going inside. He watched the doors swing closed behind them. One wore a plainsman's hat, the other was bareheaded.

They were thirsty and had to be as hungry as he was. Their overworked mounts looked about ready to collapse. How men could walk away from beasts that had served them so nobly, no oats, not even grama, only the trough, mystified him. A man on the run was only as good as his horse.

They wouldn't be going anywhere for awhile, he decided. He walked his horse to the livery stable. A lamp glowed in the little office attached to the stable. He paid for feed and keep "till I come get her, which could be soon" and a brush down. And went back to his post across from the saloon. He became fidgety; he walked over and peered over the doors. They stood at the bar; they carried on like two thirsty drovers fresh off the trail. He was tempted to haul iron, walk in, and take them, tumblers in had. Maybe order a drink himself before marching them to the marshal to hold them overnight. But the place was mobbed with innocents and women. Some of *them* might even be innocent, he thought. He would wait outside.

He went to the side alley to wait. And finished his last chaw of Battle Ax. It chased the dust coating inside his mouth. They came out about fifteen minutes later. They headed for their horses. He drew and stepped from the shadows.

"Up."

They swapped looks. One shrugged. Up went their hands.

"What's this all about, brother?" asked the taller one. He was swarthy, dark-eyed. In his veins he surely carried Mexican or Indian blood.

"Jus' inside my office here. Don' talk, just move." They did so. "Drop your belts. An' don't get cute. I'm wore to a nub; I'm everything that makes a man ornery. I'd as soon cut you down as look at you."

The taller one frowned. "You sure you got the right men?"

"Shut up."

Their belts surrounded their ankles. They stepped out of them. "What now?" asked the shorter one.

"Hand over the stone."

"What stone?"

Bert snarled. He jabbed his gun into the questioner's gut. The man yelped. "Hey, whattaya . . ."

"Let's see it."

"We got no stone," said the other.

"Turn out your pockets."

It wasn't on either.

"You . . ." He menaced the shorter one. He was jug-ugly with enormous ears that all but begged to be grabbed to lift his oversized head from his shoulders. "Get your saddlebags. Quick, before I blow his head off. I'm gettin' more tempted by the minute . . ."

The ruby was not in either set of bags.

"Where is it? I'm gettin' mad, y'hear? Gimme the damned stone!"

"I swear, brother, we don't know what you're talking about."

Bert's mind whirled. Could they have dropped it off somewhere on the way? Possibly. Anything was possible. But he doubted they'd do so. If they had, why keep riding hell bent for leather? Just to lead him on? Did they *know* he was following?

He was too tired to carry the thing further. He picked up their belts.

"Let's go, we'll go see the marshal."

"Brother, you're makin' a big mistake, honest."

"Wouldn' be the first time. MOVE!"

Marshal Ephraim Butz was too old to do much more than whittle or fish; this was Bert's impression when he walked in with his prisoners. The marshal was reading. He did not look up. His thin lips wriggled out the words as he read. He had to be closing on seventy-five. His face was deeply seamed; it displayed three days' growth of stubble. He combed what little hair he had forward ancient Roman-style; he or somebody had trimmed the ends straight across his forehead.

"Evening," he said. He still did not lift his eyes from his book.

"I'd like you to lock these two clowns up for me, Marshal."

Butz looked up for the first time. He tapped the book. *"Wild Bill, the Wild West Duelist.* All about the girl mascot of the Moonlight Mine. Exciting as all get out. General Cody write it himself, so it says. You think he can write, too? With everything else he does? I bet I've read fifteen of his books. Best was *Silk Lasso*. Ever read it?"

"It was great."

"I liked *Queen of Crater Cave*, too. Who are you? Who are they?"

Bert introduced himself; he showed his Wells Fargo I.D. And explained the situation.

"But they don't have the jewel on them," said Butz.

"They've stashed it somewheres. It'll turn up. I'll turn it up. If I got to bust bones to . . ."

"You'd best find it. It's your evidence. I can't hold 'em but overnight without you find it or something else they stole. Evidence, Mr. Slaughter, it's the track the wheels of justice run on, you know?"

"Yeah. Just lock 'em up. Please. I'll be back."

"It's almost ten-thirty. I can hold 'em till eight tomorrow morning. Be back before then. I'll be here. I'm closing up soon as I finish chapter twenty-one. Chapter twenty was a doozy. More blood than the Little Bighorn."

"I'll be back."

"Marshal," said the short, ugly one. "My name is Frank Littlejohn, this is Henry Olcott, whose daddy's a Baptist minister. We come to town from Pawnee. We was mindin' our own business. This . . ."

"Just shut up!" said Bert. "Nobody's int'rested. Marshal, I'll take full responsibility for this. It's one deep, stiff, robbery-murder case an' these two are in it up to their hair. Just you hold 'em, I'll get you your evidence."

"Eight o'clock."

"Yeah, yeah . . ."

Bert waited until Butz locked them up. He wanted to *see* the key turn in the lock before he relaxed. He thanked him and went back to the Palace. His heart was touched by the sight of the two men's horses standing patiently waiting. He walked them to the stable to be fed and brushed down. He went through the saddlebags a second time. He still couldn't find the stone.

He would get a room and leave a call for seven. First he'd have himself half a bottle of something comforting and a bite. It just might chase some of the sourness out of his system, along with the fatigue. They hadn't dropped the ruby off on their way out; they couldn't have. He kept saying so over and over to himself; he tried to sound convincing. But couldn't dismiss the possibility altogether.

He sat by himself nursing a bottle of Bolger's Goldenrod Bourbon. Vile stuff but only a buck a bottle. It might be a time before his next money from home; he would pinch what he had till it came.

Butz came in. He spotted him and sat down.

"Those two keep insisting you've made a mistake."

"They're full of it. This is rotten, you'll hate it."

"It's Bolger's, mother's milk to me."

He filled a tumbler to spilling; he bolted it down. Bert eyed him. The place was mobbed, filled with smoke and noise, piano thinkling, babbling, and the glitter of silk and sequins.

"Love it," said the marshal. He lowered his glass and gasped. "Hey, I've been meaning to ask, how will you find the ruby? You don't know anybody in town, do you? If they haven't got it on them, which they don't seem to, and they're not talking . . ."

"Sssssh. No need to tell the friggin' world . . ."

"How?" Butz lowered his voice.

"I'll find it. Could be one of 'em swallowed it. It's been done. A man'd kill to get his hands on it. They already did. It's prob'ly the biggest, most valuable ruby in the entire world. You bet they coulda' swallowed it."

The marshal whistled. He was impressed. His brow knit. "I can't stop 'em from going to the privy."

"I know . . ."

Butz downed a second tumbler full. He wished him luck in his search and left. But not before again reminding him of the eight o'clock deadline. No sooner had he walked out then a well-endowed brunette took his chair. She was not dazzlingly beautiful. Care and years sat on her features and one front tooth was graying. But her smile came easy and she seemed genuinely friendly.

"I'm not buyin'," he said. "Tapped out."

"You're not going to drink the whole bottle." She picked up the marshal's glass. She fingered out its savory wetness and licked her finger.

He grunted and poured her a little under half an inch. She sipped; she eyed him over the rim.

"What's your name?"

"Abe Lincoln."

"Hey, I voted for you."

She laughed gaily. He could not suppress a smile. An argument broke out behind him in a game of stud. Foul language; chairs scraped the floor; a fist struck bone. The two players were quickly separated.

"Boys will be boys." She offered her hand. "My name's Bedelia. Bedelia Strump. No cracks, please."

"I didn't say nothin'."

She waggled one lacquered finger. "You were about to, I could see it in your eye. Strump, not strumpet."

"What's a strumpet?"

She stared. "I like you. You're refreshing."

She was pleasant. It was like old friends meeting. They drank; Bert managed to keep her glass reasonably wet without filling it. Even a quarter full. The level in the bottle dropped slowly. Suddenly he made a face and strained forth a tight knot of a grunt.

"What's the matter?"

"My gut. I shouldn' be drinkin' on a empty stomach. Owwww." He sucked in his breath sharply.

She frowned sympathy; she half rose from her chair. "Hurts bad, doesn't it? Where 'bouts?"

"My gut, my gut..."

"High up? Low?"

"All over." He jammed his fists hard against his stomach; he doubled over and groaned again. People nearby stopped talking and stared.

"You need a doctor."

"Whatta ya think it could be?"

"I don't know, maybe appendicitis."

"Could be the Bolger's! Wouldn' you know? I mean, wouldn' you! This is all I need..."

She got up. "You're coming up to my room. I'll put you to bed and get the doctor."

"Bed maybe, no doctors. I hate 'em with a passion. All they do is bungle an' overcharge. Don' trust a one. I'm my own. I got a can o' quinine powder in my saddlebags down at the stable. I stick my knife in it an' lick both sides. It's a sure cure for everythin'. You go..."

"On your feet; we're going to my room."

• • • •

Doctor Frizzell was too fat, too hairy, too sweaty, too talkative, too cocksure. Bert lay on the narrow bed inhaling lilac mixed with lavender. He grimaced in pain. His shirt was off, his pants lowered to the points of his hips. Frizzell held a bottle in one hand, a wad of cotton in the other. Bert despised the stench of chloroform. It too easily overpowered the lilac and lavender. He was sweating himself soaking. He groaned.

Frizzell fish-eyed him. "What are you belly-aching about? I haven't even started."

"How deep do you go in?"

"No more than a foot, why?"

"Mr. Funnybone . . ."

He sneaked a peek at Bedelia Strump. She stood in a corner, her arms folded under her impressive breastworks. Worry masked her painted features. At least I'll die with somebody caring, he thought.

"I got you just in time," said Frizzell. "You can thank the lady for saving your life."

"Thanks."

"You're welcome."

"Do you know what you're doin'?" Bert asked. "Hones' an' true?"

The look Frizzell gave him suggested he was smelling an odor even fouler than the chloroform. Bert tried to speak again, but down came the cotton. Up his nostrils shot the sickening smell. He fought for breath. He got some, got some more; he struggled to push Frizzell's arm away. He was too weak and gave it up. The room began to circle. Frizzell was talking to her. Bert couldn't make out what he was saying; his voice sounded like it was coming from the far end of a long pipe. Out he went.

•   •   •   •

The cotton which had covered his nose had somehow found its way inside his mouth; it filled it. He chewed, grimaced, and spit air. He opened his eyes; the weights sitting on his upper lids closed them. Again he forced them open and chewed. He felt nauseous. He groaned. She came quickly to his side. He looked about; Frizzell had left.

"Ohhhhhh. . . ."

"Are you okay?"

"I'm awful."

"You're pale as the sheet."

"Am I..."

"Loren says you'll be just dandy. The operation was a snap. The incision's tiny."

"What's the time?"

"About four in the morning."

He tried to rise. Pain hammered dully and a great wave of nausea rose and broke in his stomach. "Ohhhhhh."

She pushed him back down gently. "Stay put. Loren says you're to stay in bed for at least two days."

"Bullsh...I can't. I got things to do. Where's he gone to? Get him back, we gotta talk."

"Will you please relax? I've made some chicken soup. It's delicious. Everybody raves about my chicken soup."

"Lemme see where he cut."

She pulled back the sheet. Bert examined his scar; he counted eight stitches.

"It's been a rough night. You have yourself a little soup and go back to sleep. He'll be by early in the morning. You can talk to your heart's content."

"You don' savvy, you don' know what's goin' on! Look, forget him for now, it's more important I talk to the marshal. Go find him, get him up here..."

"He's home asleep. The whole town's asleep. I'll get him when he comes in in the morning. I promise."

"Get there early. Catch him 'fore he opens up. Get him over here pronto. Him an' me got to talk. It's a matter o' life an' death, hones'!"

"All right, all right. Just relax. I'll get you your soup..."

He didn't hear. His snoring drowned out her last few words.

•   •   •   •

When Doctor Frizzell stopped by just after seven-thirty, he found Bedelia up from the chair where she'd spent the night and ready to face the day. Yawning and yawning at it. Bert slept on.

Frizzell stood over him. "How's he doing?"

"Fine. Have you seen Frank and Henry?"

"Not yet, it's too early."

"*I'll* see them. We can talk through their cell window. They'll be relieved to hear it went off without a hitch. Butz is going to have to let them go; he can't hold them without evidence."

Frizzell again glanced at the sleeper. "This is delicious. I love it. You slip the powder into his drink, he comes down with cramps. I open him up, take his appendix out, stick the ruby in, sew him up. It's priceless!"

"Won't he feel it inside?"

"He won't feel a thing. It's in deep enough so no lump'll show. And not too deep it can't be gotten out. He could rub his fingers against his scar and never feel a thing."

"Won't it move around?"

"It can't. It's imbedded in solid tissue. He could carry it around for the next twenty years and never suspect. Of course he'll hardly be carrying it that long. When the boys get to San Francisco they'll get somebody to dig it out. It won't be hard."

Bert mumbled in his sleep; he licked his lips. She studied him; she shook her head slowly.

"If he only knew . . ."

Frizzell laughed lightly. "He never will. Priceless. Absolutely! I love it. Mother was right. I should have been a doctor."

Four

Ben sat on the center cushion of the davenport. His face was flushed; his cheeks were streaked with tears; his lower lip quivered. He rubbed his nose with the back of his hand, sniffled, and looked up at his father through tear stained eyes.

"She's dead, Son, we both gotta face it."

"I can't help I can't stop crying. I'm trying, I am."

"Course you are."

"How come you don't, Paw?"

"I am. My tears are inside. That's the way grownups cry, so the world can't see, you know? Believe me, Ben, I'm cryin' just as much, just as hard. But we both got to stop cryin' an' face up to it. Accept it. It's been three whole days, the grief is heavy as lead an' will be from now on, but we got to carry it. Carryin' it between us is lots better than one of us alone, isn' that so?"

Ben nodded; he glanced about the parlor. Three days before, gaily colored birthday bunting had hung over the alcove. Now black crêpe hung, ominous, sad, a grim reminder of the death in the family. In the far corner on the little square table, three of his birthday gifts sat unopened. His mother had been coming home from Kansas City. He and his father had gone down to the Wells Fargo depot to wait for the stage. It was coming nearly 1,100 miles his father reminded him; they must expect it to be late. Ben geared his mind to accept the delay, however long. But it was hard to rein his patience. Mother had been away almost seven weeks. Grandmother Finley had died and they'd had the funeral. Mother had helped arrange things; now she was on her way home at last.

Then the word came flashing over the telegraph key. The stage had been held up outside of Cedar City, Utah. The driver, shotgun messenger, and a passenger had been killed. They'd first said that the passenger was an elderly woman. Then corrected it. She was young. She was Mother. A man later identified as Rance Cutler had shot her in cold blood.

On Ben's seventh birthday. Now, three days later, father and son had come back from her funeral to a house filled with sympathetic friends and neighbors. The last of them, Mr. and Mrs. Rowley who lived next door, had just left.

"We'll get through this, Ben. B'lieve me we will . . ."

"Mmmmm."

"We'll make it. Other folks lose loved ones an' live through the grief an' pain an' come out of it. We can too. Hungry?"

"Nope."

"How's 'bout a nice col' glass o' lemonade? There's still near half a pitcher full. Miz Rowley brought it over." Ben shook his head. "Don'tcha wanna open up the rest o' your birthday presents?"

"I forgot all about them. Forgot it was my birthday even."

"Open 'em up, why don'tcha?"

"Maybe later."

Fresh tears started down his cheeks. He wanted to stop crying more than anything. He couldn't. He felt like a baby in front of his father; still he couldn't stop. Bert eyed him. He gave him his handkerchief. Ben wiped his eyes and blew his nose. Loudly. A ridiculous honk. His father smiled. Ben avoided his eyes and buried his face in his hands.

• • • •

Ben and the two Belgians had turned the prisoners over to the nearest U.S. marshal in Leavenworth. Bert got Bedelia to wire Ben care of the Western Union office in the Reno

General Store. Ben had come back after helping deliver Orland, Jethro, and the others. Bert's message brought him up to date. Ben wired back that he was on his way.

Bert sat in Marshal Butz's office; he complained about his lot in life. Butz was sympathetic but he defended his freeing the prisoners.

"I told you eight o'clock."

"I was flat on my back, for Godsakes! Helpless. You coulda' at least sent somebody over to see what was goin' on."

"Over where? How was I supposed to know you were up in Bedelia Strump's room?"

"You coulda' looked for me."

"That's all I've got to do. Bert, I'm sorry about your appendix. Speaking of which, who took it out?"

"Doc Fizzle."

"Who? You don't mean Loren Frizzell..." Butz threw back his head and roared laughter. "That's rich..."

Bert had bitten off the first chaw from a fresh plug of Battle Ax. He began chomping. "Cut that out. You sound like a friggin' billy goat!"

Butz sobered. "I expect it makes sense if you think about it. The nearest genuine doctor is over in Vesper. A good thirty miles from here. It *was* an emergency..."

Bert blanched. "You mean that guy isn' a doctor?"

"He's a vet."

Bert gaped. Shock and wonderment spread over his face. He swallowed and stared for a full five seconds before he found his voice. "My God..." His hand sneaked to his scar.

"Relax. What you didn't know didn't hurt you, right? Don't get scared, Loren's perfectly capable. He's probably taken out five hundred appendices." He snickered. "Horses, cattle, sheep...."

"Shut up! If I die it'll be on your head, wise guy..."

"Me? I had nothing to do with it."

"You, her, this whole broken-down town. The nerve o' that son of a gun, cuttin' into a human bein'!" He gasped. "Come to think of it I didn' even see him wash his hands. He coulda' just come from operatin' on a pig. I could come down with hog fever! I could . . .''

"Oh, cut it out. You feel okay, don't you?"

Bert scowled, aimed, spit, and missed the spittoon. "I feel rotten!"

"Nobody told you to get up the next day."

"I see that quack, I'll hand his head to him!"

As if on cue, the door opened and in walked Frizzell. "Hello, hello . . .'' He held a piece of paper up before Bert. "I had no idea where to send this. Lucky I spotted you through the window. It's my bill. Ten dollars. A bargain, if you don't mind my saying so."

Butz laughed and laughed and laughed. Even as he restrained Bert.

• • • •

The bottom had dropped out. Bert was convinced of it. The Dragon's Eye was gone; Littlejohn and Olcott were gone. He was so weak he could hardly put one foot after the other; he could be dead before morning.

He had paid Frizzell and stalked out of the office. He went looking for Bedelia Strump; he intended to give her a large piece of his mind, but on the way over to the saloon his dander lowered. By the time he got there, he had lost all desire to tell her off. Butz had mentioned that the nearest "genuine" doctor was thirty miles away in Vesper. If she'd gone to get him, by the time she got back his appendix could have burst.

She wasn't at the Palace. The bartender told him she wasn't expected until sundown. Bert left. He stood in front of the batwing doors chewing. Mulling over his next move. Fate had really been treating him shabbily lately, he thought. Fate must have heard; she suddenly smiled. Up the street astride their mounts came Littlejohn and Olcott. He spotted them before they saw him. He backed behind the doors and to one side, eyeballing them as they passed.

"The nerve o' them lyin' snakes. Come sashayin' back into town without battin' a eye. You'd think they owned the ground they're ridin' on. But why come back here? Unless they think I'm out lookin' for 'em. An' they'll be safe here. Hey, that's it!''

They dismounted at the general store and went inside. Five minutes later they came out. What, if anything, they had purchased, he couldn't guess. They rode away in the direction they'd come from: west.

Bert ignored his sore side and hurried down to the stable. The man saddled his horse and helped him up. Sitting saddle didn't hurt as much as he figured it would. He crossed his fingers; he hoped he could ride full gallop.

Half a mile out of town he blessed Kansas for its flatness. A mile ahead, their dust rose against the white sky. Given the present terrain, he could follow them from five miles back if need be. It would take Ben another day, maybe two, to get to Gypsum. In the meantime he could get lucky. Follow them until they stopped, surprise and corral them, and fetch them back to town. Butz would keep them locked up this time. He'd see to that.

As he thought of the town, disgust rose in his gut. What a dump! When he'd first ridden in, the first thought that struck him as that every board on every building had been blown loose by the wind and nailed back on. Out of line. If a man-sized tornado ever found its way into town, it would blow on through and take every shingle with it. Loren B. Frizzell's DVM shingle hanging out front of the cottage across from the livery stable for sure.

"A vet. Jeez. . . .''

Littlejohn and Olcott showed no sign of stopping. They rode at a leisurely gait. Was one or the other carrying the ruby? He'd made them turn out their pockets in the alley; he'd searched their saddlebags. Twice. That didn't mean anything; they could drop it down a boot or the tall one, Olcott, stash it under his hat. Littlejohn didn't wear one.

They had it. The closer he drew to them, the more he felt it. As if it was giving off rays and as he rode on he was coming within range of them. He could almost feel their heat.

Another type of heat nettled him: the heat generated by Ben's wire to James B. Hume. Not to mention the Belgians' to their embassy, their capitol back home, Washington. Along about now half the law types in the country would be jumping into the hunt. In three days it could turn into a coast-to-coast carnival. And the more people taking part, the messier it would get. He sighed.

A stretch of willows broke the flatness ahead. Their dust rose above the treetops. Three riders came toward him. Closer and closer they drew; at last he could make out their faces. They were one face under three disreputable-looking hats, brims flapping. Eyes like raisins thrust deep into well-kneaded dough; hog noses; mean-looking mouths. He raised a hand in greeting. The McPig brothers out for their afternoon canter, he thought. The lead rider pulled his horse up sharply. It lifted its forehooves and whinnied protest.

"It's him!"

They quickly surrounded him; the one who had pointed him out seized his reins.

"Leggo my gear, pig face!"

Another drew his gun. "You comin' quietlike, Ernest Drysdale, or would you ruther out col' an' wakin' up with a bump on your haid?"

"You got the wrong guy."

"You tryin' to say you ain't Ernest Drysdale?" asked the third and youngest. "You sure 'nough look like him, 'ceptin' your hair."

"It's him, all right," said the one holding his reins. "No mistakin' that face."

"You're wrong! You're all screwed up. Gimme my reins an' get outta' my way. You want trouble, I'll give you a peck." The man with the reins snarled, drew, and planted his muzzle squarely between Bert's eyes. "Hey, watch it!"

"Iff'n it were up to me, Ernest Drysdale, I'd pull this here trigger an' blow your brain into the ditch. You're lucky it ain'; your lucky baby sister Ernestine is sittin' back home cryin' her purty eyes out, carryin' on to beat the band, hopin' an' prayin' we find you an' fetch you back for the nuptials."

"The what?" Bert swallowed hard; fear suddenly saturated him.

"You heerd Lamarr," said the brother alongside the gun

wielder. "Let's go!" He snatched Bert's .45 from its holster and away they went.

● ● ● ●

They rode almost two miles to a soddy with a sagging roof. Bert kept insisting they had the wrong man every step of the way.

"I'm not this Ernest What's-his-name. I never heard of him. Never seen any o' you before. Or her. You're all screwed up. It's mistaken identity, you hear? Will you stop pointin' that friggin' iron at me! You're makin' me nervous!"

"He could be tellin' the truth, Lamarr," said the youngest.

"He's lyin' in his horse teeth. He's just dyed his hair an' mustache to make himself look dark. Got a mite skinnier, but heck almighty, he's been gone near two weeks. A man could lose twenty pound easy in two weeks."

"It's him, Alton," said the other. "I'd reckynize him anyplace."

"You're fulla' bull!" said Bert. "Will you look at my I.D. card?" He continued shoving it in front of Lamarr's face. "Look at my picture, my name, my job. You must know Wells Fargo; everybody does. Does Ernest What's-his-name work for Wells Fargo? Does he?"

"Save your breath, Ernest Drysdale. For Ernestine. Here we are." He waggled a filthy finger in Bert's face. "Jus' calm down, we don' want you upsettin' lil' sister. You've got her upset 'nough as it is. You be a good boy, a gennelman, els'n I'll kick your cods off, you savvy?"

"You're makin' the biggest mistake o' your misbegotten lives!"

The house was the product of a grasshopper plow. It gently turned over a uniform slip of sod five to six inches thick and a foot or more wide. This was chopped into squares and laid like bricks. It was a calculated eyesore. Two deep-set, wooden windows penetrated the wall on either side of the door. The ridgepole rested on the sod peaks of the two gable ends. Planks ran from it to the top of the front and back walls.

The roof was a riot of wildflowers and weeds. Inside, Bert knew, like all sod houses, bugs, spiders, field mice and chunks of dirt regularly dropped into soup bowls and washbasins. Into bed and breakfast. It was not the Palace Hotel in San Francisco. It was more of an above-the-ground cave complete with earthen odors, plant and animal life, and the ever-present threat of ceiling collapse.

Home.

Lamarr threw open the door. He pushed Bert inside with his iron. The place smelled as musty as a crypt. Crudely fashioned furniture sat about. Pots and pans hung from wooden pegs in the kitchen walls. The kitchen was separated from the front room by a single long plank. One end was supported by a barrel, the other jammed into the sod wall. A man sat in a chair in the center of a rag rug in the middle of the dirt floor. He was dressed in a wedding gown; he clutched a handful of wilted wildflowers. On second look it wasn't a man; it was a girl in her late teens; her face was exactly like her brothers'. Bert had seen consistency in looks in many families but never such consistency with such godawful homeliness. In his day he had seen better looking pigs. Ernestine took one look at him, threw up her hands and corsage, burst into tears, and began to wail fit to split his eardrums. Lamarr and Alton ran to her.

"Honey love, it's him, Ernest Drysdale," said Lamarr.

"Your fancy!" said Alton.

"T'ain't nuther, you jackasses! You blind? Cain't you see? He's not my Ern!"

"I been tryin' to tell 'em," said Bert.

"He is too," said Lamarr. "A mite skinnier an' with his hair an' mustache dyed with stove blackin', but it's him."

"It's him, Ernestine darlin' dear," said a deep voice behind Bert.

He turned slowly. Attired in a worn and shining swallow-tailed coat, a beaver hat perched on his head, his white hair flowing out from under it, stood the brood's father. No mistaking the face.

"It's Ernest Drysdale sure as you're born, darlin' dear."

Bert burst into spirited protest. Up came the man's hand. Bert stopped short.

"Boy, iff'n it war up to me I'd kick you to death. But it ain't. You're bespoke to Ernestine here an' you an' her is gonna be wed as planned. Ewart."

"Yes, Paw?"

"Get on your horse. Ride over an' fetch the Reverend Belcher. Fast."

"Yes, sir."

Ewart fled.

"Paw," said Alton, "why Amos Belcher? He ain' a real preacher. Jest says he is. Walkin' 'round babblin' from the scripture, pretendin'..."

"He's the closest thing they is in this corner o' the county to a real sin-buster. He'll make a hones' woman outta Ernestine Stonecifer 'fore this day is out. Hones'," he repeated. He glared pitchforks at Bert.

"BAAAAAAAAAAAA!" wailed the bride-to-be.

"Hush up, darlin' dear."

"He ain' my Ern. I got eyes, I can see."

"Don' matter," said Alton. "He's as good as. He'll do to marry."

"He's Ernest Drysdale!" said Lamarr through his sister's caterwauling. "Tell her, Paw. Shut her up for Chrissakes."

Out flew Stonecifer's hand. It cracked against his cheek.

"WHAT'D I TELL YOU 'BOUT CUSSIN', YOUNG-UN? WHAT'D I SAY?"

"Paw..."

"Shut up an' keep shut, if you don' want I wallop the tar out'n you!"

Bert watched them. Then his attention drifted back to his intended. She wasn't just overweight a hundred pounds as he'd thought at first. She was at least seven months pregnant. She was ugly; a disaster. She eyed him blubbering; snot glistened under one fat nostril. Her wedding gown was filthy. Ancient. One lace cuff hung by a thread. The skirt was a mass of winkles.

A dirty, filthy wedding dress on his bride on this, his wedding day.

"Lord. What did I ever do to you?"

• • • •

The "Reverend" Amos Belcher weighed about 85 pounds with a rock in his pocket. He barely came up to Stonecifer's shoulder; Stonecifer barely came up to Lamarr's. Like Stonecifer, Belcher wore a stovepipe hat and swallow-tailed coat. His was not as shabby. He carried a battered Bible and the look of authority. He came trudging toward them in boots two sizes to large, Ewart by his side. Bert, the father of the bride, Lamarr, and Alton stood in front of the house. Ernestine stuck to her chair; she had retrieved her corsage of bird's foot violets, white yarrow, and creamy, green-white, tuft-flowered lace. She had reduced her wailing to a wet, sniffling whimper. She quietly mumbled continued protest that "he ain' my Ern."

At least the two of them knew it, thought Bert. Alton had said it all just after Ewart left to get Belcher: it didn't matter *who* she married, as long as she did. He would do. Another thought crossed Bert's mind as the two neared them. They all had another good reason for mistaking him for Ernest Drysdale; all had the same tiny, deep-set, black, button eyes and whenever any of them looked his way they squinted. Nearsightedness must run in the family. Except for Ernestine; she had seen at once that he wasn't her intended.

Irony crowned the whole mess. Father and daughter *expected* the boys to bring the bridegroom back. Both had dressed in their best for the ceremony. And within minutes the knot would be tied.

"I jus' had me a serious operation, you know," said Bert to Stonecifer.

The man blanched. "You mean you cain't . . ."

"No, nothin' like that. My 'pendix. It burst on me an' I lay at death's door for near two weeks. Took three doctors to save my life. Never will be hunnert percent again; too weak to lift or carry. I doubt I'll even be up to hoein' a bean patch."

"Orson," said Belcher, "how be you?" He extended his

claw and shook Stonecifer's hand. "Lovely day for a weddin',
ain't it? Where's the blushin' bride?"

"Inside, Amos. This here's my son-in-law to be, Ernest
Drysdale. Him an' his brothers got a spread over to Pocalo.
Shake hands with the Reverend Belcher, boy."

He laid a friendly hand on Bert's shoulder; Bert shook it
off. He curled his lip.

"Reverend," he said, "this is all a big mix-up. My name's
Bert Slaughter. I'm with Wells Fargo . . ."

Stonecifer twirled his finger at his temple. "Don' pay him
no mind, Amos. Altar jitters."

Belcher grinned and nodded. Stonecifer squeezed Bert's
arm. "I got me a paper dollar jus' dyin' to get spent. Shall
we get on with the cer'mony?"

Bert groaned inwardly; his heart dropped a notch in his
chest. Stonecifer still had firm hold of his arm. With the
others they started back into the soddy. A shot cracked. The
slug slammed into the sod slice above the door. The Stonecifers
flew into action. The three boys hurled themselves to the
ground. They returned fire blindly, wildly. Stonecifer jerked
Bert inside. The Reverend Belcher followed; he slammed the
door. He was petrified with fear.

"What in thunderation . . ."

"Don' pay no mind. It's them damn Georgia trash, the
Wheelocks. They's still sore on accounta' Lamarr shootin'
their heifer. By acciden'. Back las' fall. You'd think by now
they'd forgive an' forgit, stupid crackers!"

At sight of Bert, Ernestine resumed wailing. And dropped
her flowers again.

"Shut up, Ernestine darlin' dear!" said her father. She
continued louder.

Belcher ducked as glass shattered barely a foot to his right.
Lead hammered the door. Stonecifer ran to the broken window.

"Give it to 'em, boys! Shoot 'em down like dogs! KILL!
KILL!"

It was suddenly a small war. Stonecifer ran to the kitchen;
he got down a squirrel gun. He ran to the window and poured
shots at the attackers. Ernestine screamed; she slipped from
her chair; she lay on the floor kicking and blubbering. Belcher

took refuge under the table down on his knees, covering his head with his Bible. Bert crouched; he edged toward the window on the far side. A stray shot smashed it just as he got there. Shards fell down on his hat. He winced and chanced a glance out. Two men were down behind convenient piles of dirt; they poured lead at the three brothers. Lamarr was hit; he yelled in pain. Alton edged toward him; he stopped short as two slugs kicked dirt inches from his face.

Bert looked about. Stonecifer had reloaded; he resumed firing. Ernestine continued to kick, blubber, and wail. Belcher was still doubled under the table. Bert sneaked a look out the window. Just in time to see one of the attackers raise up and fire, let fly, and drop to safety, all in a second and a half.

He edged toward the rear of the house. He passed Ernestine, still on the floor kicking. He moved around the barrel holding up the plank shelf. He jerked open the back door and ran out. He paused and pulled it quietly closed. A blast ripped a hole dead-center the door; it missed his ribs by a hair. All the horses except Ewart's and the one Belcher had ridden in on were tied in back. His own among them. His hand strayed to his empty holster as he ran toward his horse. The heck with it, he thought, he could pick up a gun someplace.

He mounted and started off. The back door flew open. Stonecifer aimed his squirrel gun. He yelled, threatened, cursed, fired, and missed.

On and on rode Bert until the soddy had shrunk to the size of his thumbnail. A rectangular silhouette poking through the horizon under the setting sun.

His thoughts flew back. Once more he was looking out the window; he caught sight of one of the attackers. With the sun at his back, he couldn't make out his face. But he wore no hat. He could see that his ears were usually large. They protruded like jug handles. No, more like the grips of beer steins. Stonecifer had mentioned Georgia crackers, the Wheelocks, but those ears looked very familiar. Looked exactly like Frank Littlejohn's.

But it couldn't have been him. Impossible. By now he and Olcott had to be miles away.

Five

Bert arrived in the first town west of Gypsum; he was wrung out and hurting bad. Sand City was like a thousand other towns scattered about the Great Plains: no more impressive than Reno, no less than Gypsum. The sameness of them all was discouraging. Always the ever-present false fronts confronting each other across a street as wide as a field. The same buildings in size and nearly number. The same overall grayness, as if color was taboo. When he took in the view, it struck him that such places had been thrown up as temporary hamlets. Stopping off places for westbound emigrants. Clapboard and shakeboard camps that should have been abandoned years before. When the railroad came by and speeded travel across the land, many *had* been abandoned, bypassed, left to rot, and eventually collapsed in the dust. The further one penetrated into western Kansas, the sparser and poorer the towns became. The thinner the mattresses, the cheaper and fouler the liquor, the fewer the luxuries, the drabber the lives.

The Union Pacific ran through Sand City. But it seemed to have done little for it, apart from keeping it going. No station, only a wooden platform, the planks laid crosswise; they bent up slightly at the corners, fighting the grip of the nails. A small toolshed tilted slightly on its foundation. Across the tracks twenty yards up the way stood the water tank. "Sand City" was painted on it in enormous, faded red letters. Beyond the tank the sun burned into the Smoky Hills. Shadows spilled back down the tracks.

A chair was tilted against the toolshed. In it a man sat snoring. He wore bibs that looked as if they'd been dragged through a hog wallow; he wore a straw hat. It covered his face and muffled his snore. A sprig of alfalfa sneaked out from under his hat brim. A partially stove-in eggcrate supported his long legs stretched out in front of him. His feet were bare; his boots sat side by side next to them. Ben approached. *If* Littlejohn and Olcott had kept to the way he was following, they would have come to Sand City. He had looked for their horses: a small bay mare with a speckled rump and a black-as-pitch mustang. Common enough horseflesh, but seen together proof they were here. He had not see them. If they *had* ridden in, they could have boarded a train, horses and all. They could also have bypassed the town—cut north or south well before it. They could be on their way to the Nebraska border. Or south to Oklahoma.

The Stonecifers had taken a lot of the little he had left out of him. Losing Littlejohn and Olcott irked him. Now, here he was, stuck out in the middle of nowhere. Out of contact with Ben, hurting, beat down to his heels.

"'Scuse me. Hey, wake up. HEY!''

The man under the hat sniffed. He cleared his throat and licked his lips. Up came the brim. "You woke me up."

"Sorry, it's important. How long you been here?"

"Where you get off wakin' a man up outta' a sound sleep?"

"I said I was sorry. When did the last train come through?"

"This morning."

"When's the next?"

"Eleven o'clock tonight, why?"

The wind flattened the grass on the far side of the racks. Dust whirled briefly, then settled. The day was an oven even now, at sunset. Bert glanced down the platform.

"Where do you buy your ticket?"

"On the train, what do you think? Never has been no station here." He yawned and spoke through it. "Go 'way and leave me sleep." Down came his hat brim.

"Just one more question. You see anythin' o' two fellows, one short, ugly as sin with great big ears stickin' straight out? The other . . ."

"Go 'way!"

"Please."

"BEAT IT!"

He snored. Pretended he was asleep. No way could he get back to sleep so quickly.

"Hey . . ."

It was useless. Bert was tempted to kick his legs off the crate. He fought back the urge. He started off leading his horse; he stopped, came back, picked up one of the boots, and flung it across the tracks into the tall grass. He grit his teeth as he did; and stifled a yelp of pain. The man snored on. Bert gingerly felt of his scar as he walked off. He undid his shirt. One end of the adhesive had come loose. He lifted it; he had jerked three stitches loose; tiny beads of blood glistened. He swore. He refastened the adhesive and rebuttoned his shirt. The dull soreness gave way to a stinging.

To hell with it, he thought. To hell with those two, the Dragon's Eye, Wells Fargo. To hell with Gypsum, Sand City, the world.

"A man only got so much to give an' I give all I got. Quittin' time."

He hitched in front of the Sand City Diner–Steaks Our Specialty. The place smelled of fried onions. It was too early for the supper crowd. He sat alone at the counter, his hat on it, his chin on his palms. The sting in his stitches persisted. He was exhausted, but it would keep him awake. He'd take a bottle to bed; the sting in his throat would offset his side. He shook his head. What a life.

The waitress was in her sixties: small, almost frail looking; motherly looking. Neatly pinned-up white hair. Pretty, pale-blue eyes exactly the color of Ben's. They gleamed behind gold-filled spectacles. She was a little bird fussing about the counter. She chased crumbs with a flick of her napkin. She straightened the salt and papper shakers. And lay a knife and fork in front of him.

"What'll it be?"

"Steak an' onions."

"Take your hat off the counter."

"What for?"

"It's not sanitary."

He eyed the counter. "Looks clean to me."

He set his hat on the stool beside him. A man and woman came in. They carried on like two schoolchildren. She poked him playfully. They sat at the far end. The waitress glided down to them carrying water; she had not given Bert any. She greeted them. So friendly Bert wondered if they were kin. The locals get the smiles, the strangers scowls and no water.

She set his steak down. Like the planks of the depot platform, the ends curled up slightly from under a slab of fried onions. He had to saw to start his cut. He gave up and went to his Green River knife. It he kept sharp enough to shave with. It had a hard time making it through the sinew. He separated a small chunk and began chewing. It defied mastication. Chomp, chomp, chomp barely dented it. He gripped one end of it and tried to shred a piece loose. He did and chewed and chewed. He finally gave up and swallowed it whole.

"Hey..."

The waitress was back down at the far end talking with the couple. She was giggling. She lit the man's cigar for him.

"I said hey!"

The man called her attention to Bert. She frowned.

"What now?"

"Whatta ya mean, now? Wouldja come down here a second, please?"

She approached. "What is it?"

"This is no steak, this is fried rock."

She stood directly in front of him. Down snapped her head. She lowered her face to within an inch of the steak. A hairpin dropped onto it. She picked it up and shoved it back into her hair. Up came her face. Her eyes challenged.

"Looks all right to me..."

"It *looks* aces."

"How's it taste?"

"I dunno. It's so tough I can't cut it. A Wostenholm razor couldn' cut it. It's solid sinew."

"Looks all right to me . . ."

She had looked motherly before; now she looked like a witch with glasses. She set her jaw; her eyes stabbed at him; her voice took on a tone that put him in mind of a fingernail scraping down a blackboard. She worked her skinny fingers as if readying them to lay hold of his neck and strangle him.

"Lady, it's a bum cut from a bum steer. I couldn' chew it if I had stove bolts for teeth. I couldn' digest it if I swallowed it. Can you please take it away an' bring me some eggs, maybe some toast?"

"Looks all right to me . . ."

"Take it away!"

"Everything all right, maw?"

The man at the other end stood up. He looked a foot taller than when he came in. He came striding up; his companion followed.

"This bozo claims his steak's too tough, Howard. I don't serve tough steaks."

"Looks all right to me . . ."

Bert threw up his hands; he pulled his stitches; he stifled a yelp. He got up and left without another word to either. To himself he blabbed without letup. Still upset, still muttering, hungrier than ever, he stood outside away from the window, out of sight of mother and son. A lone rider came loping into town.

"BEN!"

●　●　●　●

They sat at a table in the little restaurant snugged up to Grosvenor's Sand City Saloon. The tablecloth was wrinkled, smudged, and yellow with age. Bert's chair was harder than a railroad seat. The clamor of the diners was magnified by the low ceiling. The window looking into the street needed scraping before it could be washed. The waitress looked as if she had been up three nights in a row. The steak was hot, tender, and delicious. Bert wolfed it down. Ben admitted he had contacted Hume in San Francisco.

"Did you have to?"

"Absolutely."

"You coulda' at least held off till end o' the week. Now every jackass with a badge an' a gun'll be jumpin' in. Ain' we got trouble enough without turnin' it into a three-ring circus?"

"Relax, we'll catch up with them before anybody else does."

"I already did. An' lost 'em. They're gone for good this time. Got to be. Lightnin' luck don' strike but once. I've had nothin' but one rotten break after another since Gypsum. Talk about jinx towns. I near died on that operatin' table. When I come outta' the chloroform, the doc tol' me it was the toughest operation he ever performed. Bigges' 'pendix he ever saw. I was at death's door. Within a inch o' fallin' through. Lucky I got the constitution of a bull. Cast-iron guts. Only thing pulled me through. Still hurts something fierce, but you know me, I can stand pain ten times as good as the next fella."

"I'm sure. You should have stayed in bed. It's customary after an operation. It's called recuperating."

"I'm okay. I mean I don' mind the sufferin'. It was them Stonecifers wore me down."

"How could they ever mistake you for the girl's fiance?"

"They was all half-blind from nearsightedness. Except her. I'll say one thing, Ben, she was a beauty. Long, glistenin' hair, black as a grackle's wing. Prettiest, purest face; eyes so big an' soft an' warm you just want to jump into 'em. An' some beautiful figger; she was a livin' angel. What she was doin' with that buncha' devils I'll never know. A pearl 'mong swine. An' she sure went for me. She'd turn that golden smile on me . . . Yes sir, she was some desir'ble creature, you betcha. You'da' lost your heart for fair if you saw her."

Ben sighed and shook his head.

"What's the matter?"

"My hat's off to you. Nobody I know can hold a candle to you."

"For what?"

"How can you lie so outrageously? And look me straight in the eye while you're doing it? Doesn't your conscience bother you?"

"What lie, what are you talkin' about? Her? You don't think a beautiful woman would find me desir'ble? Heck, there's young girls purely love older men."

"Enough, please. Finish your steak."

"What's the rush? Hey, how'd you know I come here?"

"Marshal Butz. When I got to Gypsum I looked for you. I checked with him. He said the last he'd see you were heading west out of town. I figured you must be chasing them. When I got here I spotted your horse."

"Mmmmm. Ben."

"What?"

"This thing has turned into one towerin' mess. Everything that could has gone wrong."

"When you had them in jail in Gypsum, did either give you any idea where they might be heading?"

"We didn't talk about that. All I cared about was the Dragon's Eye. Didn't neither have it on 'em. They got to have stashed it somewheres in town."

"Why do you say that?"

"Hunch."

"Marvelous."

Bert stiffened. "My hunches are good, the best. They come outta' experience, instincts. Think about it: if you were them, would you keep runnin', carryin' it on you? Knowin' you were bein' chased? Knowin' you could be caught up with anytime? No sir, you'd give it up, like they did after two days an' nights runnin'. You'd drop it off somewheres safe, figgerin' you could come back anytime."

"I disagree. Why complicate things unnecessarily? Besides, they didn't steal it to hang it over the mantelpiece. They've got a buyer for it. Which means they've got a schedule to keep." He paused; he eyed his father. "You're in no shape to keep going."

"I'm aces."

"You can hardly keep your eyes open. Your incision hurts,

doesn't it? Those torn stitches should be replaced. There's no sense risking infection.''

"I only got three loose. Still five holdin' me together. I can walk. I can mount, ride.''

"Let's go back to Gypsum.''

"What for?''

"Didn't I just hear you say the stone is there?''

"I said I had a hunch . . .''

"Well I've got a hunch myself. To pick up the chase now, with so much time elapsed, is a waste of energy. I'm afraid it's all over.''

Down came the flat of Bert's hand. It slammed and jiggled the table. "IT'S NEVER ALL OVER! WHAT'S THE MATTER WITH YOU?!''

"Ssssh, for heaven's sakes . . .''

"Give up if you want to, not me. I'm goin' on. I'll find 'em if I got to track 'em to Alaska!''

• • • •

Butz closed his copy of *Buffalo Bill Cody and the Black Hood Gang*. He measured Bert.

"You look half-dead.''

"Shut up.''

"Maybe even three-quarters. What did you do, chase them and lose them? You did, didn't you?''

"Marshal,'' said Ben. "When you had them here did they say anything? Did they let slip where they might be heading? They didn't did they?'' he added. He sighed.

"So whatta ya askin' him for?''

Butz grinned. Bert glared. "Brace yourselves,'' said the marshal. "I got good news. Just after you left . . .'' He nodded toward Ben. "Two of your people showed up.''

"The Belgians?''

"Two Wells Fargo detectives. A Mr. Crowley and some other fellow. I don't recall his name. They're over at the Palace washing the dust out of their throats.'' He sat upright; he looked past Ben out the window. "Here they come.''

Father and son looked out.

"Mace Crowley an' Wardell Hubbard," said Bert. "Son of a bucket!"

"Which one?" asked Butz.

Ben cleared his throat. "My father and Mr. Hubbard are old acquaintances."

"I hate him an' he hates me. Damn gossipy ol' hen. Jackass in muttonchops. Biggest pain in the butt in the whole outfit. Everybody hates him. Knows it all. Listens to nobody. Kisses Lloyd Tevis's rear an' every other in sight like a baby goin' after a sugar cookie. What luck, a hunnert an' sixteen men on the payroll an' Ol' Mother Hubbard's got to turn up here. Mace Crowley, he's a saint. Takes a saint, takes Job himself to work with that simple-minded, flannel-mouthed son of a bucket!"

"Calm down," said Ben. "You'll snap another stitch. Don't start up with him. They're here to help."

"Thanks to you. You had to wire Hume. Couldn't wait. Asked for help, didn't you? Here it comes, Ol' Mother Hubbard!" He cursed, threw up his hands, pulled his stitches, and bellowed pain.

In walked Crowley and Hubbard. Mace Crowley was handsome, distinguished looking. He boasted wavy black hair and a theatrical profile that turned many a female head when he walked down the street. He wore his good looks modestly; he was a capable and hardworking member of the force. He had been a Pinkerton operative before coming to Wells Fargo. In Bert's opinion, he was the only man out of the 116 who could work with Hubbard.

Hubbard had none of his partner's good looks. He was stumpy, a round little man with a mouth too wide for his face. Too loud for his listeners. His complexion was as ruddy as a ripe peach. He looked as if he'd been standing on his head and all his blood had descended to it. At times Bert called him Turnip. Mace greeted both Slaughters. The best Hubbard could do was a curt double nod.

"Well, well, well, well, well." He leered at Bert. "Here we are."

"Ain' it the truth."

"Arrived in the nick of time to pull your chestnuts out of

the fire. You've outdone yourself this time, Slaughter. I don't suppose you have a clue as to their whereabouts, much less the ruby's. The wheels have been turning while you've been floundering. The government's posted a ten-thousand-dollar reward, President Grant has given the company one week to recover the stone—two days you've already squandered. Five more and Wells Fargo is formally fired. The newspapers will start pillorying us, our competition will snicker and cheer, and we'll all be walking around with red faces. In will come the army, the navy, and every man west of the Mississippi wearing tin. There'll be holy hell to pay in Antwerp, Washington, San Francisco. Chief Hume threw an apoplectic fit when he heard. Do you blame him? Well, let's have it, what's going on? What have you done? Where do we stand?''

"Nowheres.'' Bert yawned in his red face. "Go on home an' count your toes, why don'tcha? Leave them that know what they're doin' handle things.''

"And what a bang-up job you've done so far.''

Crowley laid a hand on his arm. "Easy, Ward.''

"FACTS! That's what we want to hear. The who, the where, what, how . . .''

"Mace, the stone's right here in town. Give me a hour an' I'll have it in my hand. As for the two who took it, once we get *it* back, we'll pick them up easy as chestnuts off the ground. Everything's under control. Me an' Ben 'preciate *your* comin', Mace. It's always nice to see a old friend, but no need to stay. We're on top o' things with flyin' colors.''

"Of course you are.'' Hubbard withered him with a glare. "We just dropped by to watch you mop up. Indulge us, let's see you in action. We can always learn from the old master.'' His expression hardened. "You know where it is? Capital!'' He stood aside; he swept his arm toward the door. "Lead us to it.''

"I got a better idea. You boys go back to the saloon. Get a table, relax, we'll bring it to you.''

"Bert . . . .''

"It's okay, son. In an hour; cross my heart hope to die.''

Crowley glanced at Hubbard and shrugged. "Whatever you say, Bert.''

"WHATEVER HE SAYS?!''

"Take it or leave it, Turnip.'' Bert rose. He had a hard time steadying himself. Ben went to him. He waved him away. Hubbard stared.

"What's ailing you?''

"Nothin'. Marshal, you got a ol' iron lyin' around you could loan me?''

"Sure.''

Butz whipped open the bottom drawer of his desk. In it was a jumble of handguns: a couple of Remington Frontier .44s, an ivory-gripped Smith & Wesson American, no fewer than four Colt Frontier Double-Action .45s, a Schofield, a seven-and-a-half-inch barrel Classic Peacemaker, even an old-fashioned Starr Double-Action Army .44. Bert selected the Classic. He hefted it, examined it.

"Check and see it's loaded. Some are, some only got a cartridge or two. I can't spare any ammunition.''

The gun was loaded. "Thanks, Marshal. I'll get it back to you.''

"Keep it. The drawer's getting so full I'm going to have to start using a second one.'' He grinned. "Or hold me an auction.''

Bert waved to Mace. "Come on, Ben.''

They crossed the street.

Ben was exasperated. "Now you've done it. Why tell them you'd get the ruby back? In an hour no less.''

"It shut the turnip up. Got us outta' there an' them outta' our hair at least for now, didn' it?''

"What now?''

"How about a drink? In that other saloon. They'll likely head back to the Palace. After maybe we'll go have a little talk with Bedelia Strump; she gets around; maybe she heard somethin' about Littlejohn an' Olcott.

• • • •

They stepped up to the bar. It was early but the place was already crowded with patrons. A thinly clad odalisque re-clined on a bearskin rug above the rear mirror. Her elbow was planted between the fierce-looking creature's eyes. She smiled blankly down at them. Bert was about to voice his usual request for Haggerty's Morning Dew. Just as he opened his mouth the doors to their left squeaked. They turned.

There stood Littlejohn and Olcott. Eyes clashed. All four reacted. The outlaws fled; the Slaughters took off after them.

Six

On the pier table lay a crumpled telegram. The table was a beautiful piece; a product of the hand of the celebrated Duncan Phyfe himself. The reeding of the legs, the tight leaf carving on their upturned portions, the massive pawed feet were particularly impressive.

Lloyd Tevis, president and chief operating officer of Wells Fargo & Company, used the table as a desk. No drawers, of course, not even a blotter. No writing utensils. All such necessities Tevis relegated to his subordinates. He carried the business of the business in his head. The keeping of files, correspondence, and all else in the way of paperwork he delegated to his inferiors, down to the office boys and mailroom clerks.

His office testified to the man's exceptional taste. At the Duncan Phyfe table he sat in a late-eighteenth-century straight-backed armchair called a *fauteil a la reine*. It boasted gilt-bronze mounts and deeply buttoned gold damask fabric. A second, smaller pier table stood against a wall; an American interpretation of the French Empire style, it boasted dolphin feet and swan supports. Gilded terra-cotta rosettes and caps and bases for the columns and a surface of veneered rosewood. Other pieces were just as impressive. A magnificent Isfahan carpet overlay the hardwood floor.

Tevis combed his slightly wavy and thinning gray hair from left to right across his scalp. He displayed a salt-and-pepper, paintbrush beard which stretched across his neck on either side and ascended to a point alongside his earlobes. He wore no mustache, nor was he a snappy dresser. He was tolerably good looking, his nose aquiline. Some claimed he had a weak chin and had grown a beard to cover it. In his eyes there was no sign of weakness. When his back was up his eyes could be fierce and icy cold. Ice-eyes was Bert Slaughter's name for him. Not one addressed to him in person, but known and used by other employees behind his back. Tevis was shrewd and intelligent. In Ben Slaughter's opinion—not shared by his father—brilliant. Bert did not like Tevis. Did not like the way he had slickered Henry Wells and William Fargo out of ownership of the company they had founded back in 1852. Tevis had taken over the company, but skillfully and legally, and many admired him for his triumph.

At the moment, however, that triumph seemed somewhat hollow. To Tevis himself certainly. He had summoned Chief James B. Hume to his office to discuss what had come to be called the Belgian Tragedy. Fiasco.

"We've heard from Detectives Hubbard and Crowley from a place in central Kansas called Gypsum," said Tevis. "You were out; I took the liberty of opening the wire. They arrived and made contact with the Slaughters."

"Good . . ."

"Only to have the Slaughters run out on them. If anything 'good' is to be made of that, I fail to see it."

Hume's complexion grayed.

"You know those two better than I. You've always put great faith in them, especially the father. What do you think they're up to?"

"Maybe they got a line on the thieves. And had to follow it up. Didn't have time to apprise Crowley and Hubbard."

"Ever since the ruby was stolen, they've deliberately avoided contacting you."

"Ben wired us."

"Since then. What possible reason could they have for working in the dark?"

"Ben explained what happened in detail."

"What choice did he have? I'm talking lately, the past

three days. The president's issued us an ultimatum. We've got a week. Four days now. I think he's being generous, don't you?

"Four days left. With no word of any progress. No word of any kind. Jim, I think we should get wanted posters out on both Slaughters . . ."

"With all respect, sir, I think that's much too drastic."

"Too drastic? Very well, how do you propose to bring them back into line? Start working properly, according to the rules."

He punctuated each word with a slap on the table; the crumpled telegram jumped and jumped.

"I think they're doing their job."

"You hope."

"There are times men in the field are too busy to contact us. Between towns, in a place where the telegraph is down, where there is none. I'm sure there's a good reason why we haven't heard." Tevis rose. He picked up the telegram. "I know. Crowley and Hubbard got in touch . . ."

"Jim, I know you have a strong sense of loyalty toward all your men. It's very admirable. I'm sure in most cases it's justified. But this happens to be an unusual situation. Extraordinary. We're sitting on dynamite. If things keep on the way they're going, we could be ruined. Made the laughing stock of the industry. We could be locked in the federal doghouse and the key tossed in the Potomac. We could end up closing our doors!"

He was exaggerating. But Hume resisted the temptation to counter his argument. What could he say? He certainly couldn't reaffirm his confidence in Bert and Ben. Tevis was right on one point: one of them should be keeping in touch. Ben surprised him; he was generally very buttoned up about keeping in contact. Had something happened to prevent it? Had he been wounded? Was he dead? Were both?

Tevis cut into his thoughts. He inserted an Old Judge cigarette in his ivory holder.

"Whatever the outcome, one thing is certain. They've put us through the wringer on this; they're going to pay. Dearly. They're finished, Jim."

"Sir . . ."

"Through with Wells Fargo. This was a routine assignment: four men guarding a jewel collection locked in a safe, the safe locked in a mail car. Stolen. Oh, I know they got most of them back, but not that ruby. And you can bet your bottom dollar they haven't the faintest idea where it's gotten to. It could be out of the country. Or cut up into a hundred pieces. It could be completely reshaped to hide its identity. Anybody who gets his hands on it would willingly sacrifice some of its value to disguise it.

"I know, the Slaughters' record with the company is excellent. I don't deny it." He planted his knuckles on the table; he leaned forward, bringing his face to within inches of Hume's. His eyes were icier than ever.

"And they're well paid for it. For their services. Why should we reward them for failure to perform said services?"

"Not a man on staff has a hundred percent record of success. It's unrealistic to expect it."

"If I'm being 'unrealistic'," said Tevis, "so be it. Win, lose, or draw, those two are finished."

● ● ● ●

"About time we got a break," said Bert.

"Cross your fingers we don't lose them again."

"Oh sure, look at the bright side. You're one sour pickle, you know that? Born pessimist."

"Don't talk, you invented the word. You've got a patent on the attitude."

"The break I'm talkin' about is the stone, dummy. Why else would they come back to town but to get it, right? Tol'ja I had a hunch. I was dead right!"

"You'll be dead period if they don't stop soon."

"Baloney, I never felt fitter in my life. Change o' luck does it every time. Picks up a man's spirits, shakes out the gloom, dulls his mind to his sufferin', fills his chest with sunshine. Smile, boy, we as good as got that ruby smack dab in our fist. I can feel it pressin' my flesh, hones' to God if I can't!"

Kansas was divided into three grasses. In the east was

found the lovely and sweet-smelling bluegrass interspersed with native grasses. Next, heading west, came the Blue Stem Hills, where the distinctive cattle-fattening grasses thrived. Through them they now rode. On the high plains beyond, in the western half of the state, the bluestem surrendered the soil to buffalo grass. Alfalfa, too, did well throughout the state, and the deep green of tame hay colored the valley lands far into Colorado.

The insufferable heat was beginning to relax its grip. The air continued sweltering, but with an occasional breeze, and riding at a brisk pace had a cooling effect. Ben eyed his father askance. What a remarkable specimen he was; the sudden change in their luck had completely restored him. The color had come back to his cheeks, his eyes had lost their glazed sickly look, he was infused with life; he was his old, his usual feisty, ornery self.

What a man my father is, he thought. He closed his ears to Bert's pointless chattering and sent his mind rolling back over their years together.

The house in Rawlings, Wyoming, was smaller by two rooms than home in Stockton. They had moved to Rawlings after Mother's death; Bert had taken a job as Wells Fargo agent. There were only two bedrooms. It was dark inside during the day, the two green ashes on the front lawn blocking the sun out of the parlor. Perhaps, he recalled thinking at the time, it was only darker than the parlor in the old house because she wasn't there to brighten it. Mother. She had been the sunshine of both their lives. Always happy, sparkling, even in the grayest times; bright and chipper, eternally optimistic, the perfect counterpoise to Bert's pessimism. Rawlings was a long way from Stockton; Ben had assumed when they moved that the distance would help alleviate the pain of her loss. It hadn't.

In the days that followed her funeral he studied his father; he concluded that Bert was taking it a great deal better than he. Then he'd recall what Bert had said the day of her funeral, just after it, about his crying inside. Ben didn't believe a word of it at the time; it was only said to ease his own grief. Grown men simply didn't cry period, inside or out.

No sooner had they moved into their new home then a lonesome, yearning feeling enveloped him. The unfamiliar surroundings, strange faces, absence of friends, the whole new world of Rawlings disheartened him. And he had no desire to adapt. It would be too hard, it would be pointless. He didn't tell his father, but that was his decision. He resolved to stay clear of people, especially boys his own age. Make no friends, keep to himself, accept his loneliness and live with it as best he could.

Had his father known, he would only have objected. Down the idea, trot out all the reasons why he should get to know everyone he could, get to know Rawlings, explore it, take it in, wrap himself in it. Why be a hermit? Was it his idea of penance? For what? He wasn't to blame for his mother's death. All true; still, there were some things fathers and mothers just didn't understand, private, personal judgments and decisions that one made. Had to make. And stick to.

They had moved in in the afternoon. That night after supper Ben was in his room reading *Conquering the Wilderness; Or Heroes and Heroines of Pioneer Life and Adventure* by Colonel Frank Triplett when Bert came into his room with a yardstick.

"Got a minute?"

"Sure."

He stood him against the kitchen doorjamb. He pressed his hair down with the yardstick, then scratched the jamb exactly at his height using his penknife. He measured.

"Forty-nine an' three-quarter inches. Not bad for somebody just turned seven. Four feet almos' two inches. You're becomin' one tall drink o' water, Benjamin. By the time you're sixteen I reckon you'll be six foot six."

"Naw . . ."

"Really. I'm six-three, an' everybody knows sons outgrow their fathers. I outgrew mine. That's one o' the best known facts o' Nature there is."

By the time he left Rawlings to go east to college, the notches had ascended to six feet even. It proved to be as tall as he was to grow, but the three inches his father had on him did not show when they stood side by side. Thanks to Bert's habitually poor posture.

In his mind's eye he saw again the doorjamb and the ladder of notches. How much more than height they measured! The months, the years, eleven of them up to his eighteenth birthday. They measured the changes in his values, his thinking, his outlook on life. The healing power of time had taken its effect, the pain of their loss eased, if not memory of the cruelty of Mother's murder. That could never be anything but uppermost in both their minds.

Bert rarely mentioned Rance Cutler; when he did, it was usually when he'd had too much to drink, when every man's guard is down and his mind prey to recollection of his life's tragedies. He himself never mentioned Cutler by name, it was always "he." Curiously, his bitterness toward Cutler lessened as he moved through his years. Though not his hunger for vengeance. To him there was a distinction between the two. Bert's bitterness persisted; it seemed to become deeper with the passage of time. Become at length so powerful it consumed him. It was unhealthy; it sapped his strength, distorted his outlook, and distracted him from other things. Like work. Hume knew about Cutler. He repeatedly warned them both against carrying on their private war on company time. All their time was "company time," such was the nature of the job. When then were they supposed to deal with Cutler? Bert ignored Hume's warning; whenever chance brought Ariel's murderer within his reach, he dropped everything. It had happened three times thus far. The last time, Ben had outfoxed his father; he had deliberately thrown him off Cutler's track and taken the case up himself. He had caught up with Cutler, they had shot it out. He had disposed of Cutler's two sidekicks, but in the process lost him.

That one Bert would never let him forget. Ben knew there was no use trying to explain to him why he'd thrown him off the track: because his father's fanatical thirst for vengeance dismissed intelligence and commonsense in favor of recklessness. Mere sight of the snake and Bert's ingrained hatred seemed to demand he go off half-cocked. There'd be no time for thoughtful consideration of the situation; no time to plan suitable strategy.

Ben refused to let him be killed by his own rashness. So *he* had taken over. But failed to kill Cutler. Now Bert would never let him forget it.

God forbid he did kill Cutler; his father would probably never speak to him again!

On and on into the long, dreary, lonely hours of the heart of the night rode Littlejohn and Olcott. On rode father and son. It was not until the first, feeble, gray light of the new day that the outlaws pulled up. They veered off the road and stopped about a mile from a little town; from a distance it looked like Reno. Ben and Bert also pulled up. They dismounted behind the cover of a grass-crowned hillock. Ben felt wearier than his father looked.

"Let's get them, get this thing over with once and for all."

Bert scratched his stubbled chin; he studied the ground at his feet; he knelt, loosed a stem of hay grass, and began chewing. "We could, I guess."

"So let's go . . ."

"Hold it. They're not goin' anywheres, not right away . . ."

Ben sneaked a look around the hillock. They stood talking, the shorter one, Littlejohn, drinking from his canteen.

"Spit it out, Bert."

Bert put on his most innocent look, infusing it with a hurt expression.

"Don' be rude to your ol' man, son. It's b'neath you. I been thinkin' while I been talkin' an' you been ignorin' me. With neither of us botherin' to ring Hume in on what's been goin' on, we got to be deep in the mud up to our necks back at headquarters. Along 'bout now I'll bet him an' John Valentine an' ol' Ice-eyes are makin' up dolls of us an' stickin' rusty pins in 'em. I bet we been fired seven times over."

"Agreed. So?"

"So whatta we got to lose by followin' those two all the way to where they're goin'? To where they make their deal with whoever's gonna buy the Dragon's Eye. Catch the fella or bunch they mean to do business with. We do us the whole, complete job. Which is the way detectives are s'posed to operate.''

Ben shook his head. ''We could track them all the way to the coast, if that's where they're heading. And lose them anytime. We've already proven we know how . . .''

''Cut it out. That's jus' defeatis' talk: sour-pickle pessimism. You don' savvy what I'm sayin'. As things stand, we're dead with Hume an' the company. Even if we bring 'em in an' the stone, it'll be a miracle they don' throw us out a window.''

''Would being fired really bother you? I mean really?''

''It'd bother me somethin' fierce. It's a matter of principle, damnit!''

''Ssssh, keep it down.''

''We've had nothin' but bad breaks topped off by my 'pendicitis. Why should we be fired on accounta' bad luck? Them two Belgians were as much as fault for the train holdup as us.

''Ben, I like this job, I'd like to keep it. There aren't that many like it aroun'. I sure don' want it snatched from me an' to be thrown on the ash heap o' retirement through no friggin' fault I had any control over. But if we was to follow through, stay on their tails till they meet their contact an' grab the lot an' the ruby, we'll be back sittin' pretty. The newspapers'll eat it up. I can jus' see the headlines. Two Never-Say-Die Wells Fargo Detectives Solve King Leopole' Ruby Case Single-Handed. Criminals Apprehended. Gem Restored to His Highness. Belgian Government Rewards Father an' Son Detective Team with Distinguished Gol' Medal o' Honor!''

''My God . . .''

''Doin' the whole, complete job. Wrappin' up all the loose ends is our only chance. The company wouldn' dare fire two heroes who solved the crime o' the century, got back the bigges', most valuable ruby in the worl' an' was given a gold medal by a friggin' king! Tevis wouldn' dare!''

He couldn't have described it more melodramatically if he tried, but Ben could not fault his logic. He rarely could. They *could* take Littlejohn and Olcott here and now . . .

But what if they didn't have the ruby on them?

Again.

What if they'd mailed it to themselves, care of wherever they were heading? Wherever that might be, they'd definitely have it there; they'd have to have it when they made their deal. And, as Bert suggested, they could collar the buyer at the same time.

"I can see by the look in your eye you 'gree with me one hunnert percent!"

"Oh, shut up!"

Bert threw an arm around him. "That's my boy."

Ben didn't hear. Not really. He was thinking about the house in Rawlings again. How old it had been when they'd moved in. When he went off to college, it was one of the oldest in town. On the verge of collapse. Probably had by now.

And with it the kitchen doorjamb and the stacked up notches of his previous life.

Seven

The desk clerk at the Ophir Junction Hotel yawned greeting.
A front tooth was missing. His rat-colored hair was heavily
pomaded, plastered down on both sides of his center part. It
looked to Bert like a cleaver had scarred it. The man's eyes
were gritty with sleep, his breath reeked of garlic and he
looked like he hadn't been out of his clothes in a week; he
was friendly.

"Pleasant good evening to you, gents. Good morning, that
is."

They got a double room. They had waited outside and
watched Littlejohn and Olcott enter. And given them time to
register and go upstairs.

"I'm suddenly doing a land-office business; four guests in
two minutes." They had signed in. He swiveled the registra-
tion book back around and eyed it. "Mr. . . . Tevis, Mr. . . .
Hume. Got a nice corner room, second floor rear."

"Any chance of getting a plunge bath brought up?" asked
Ben.

"There's one in the hall closet. Water's out back. You'll
have to carry it up yourselves, I'm afraid. The porter goes off
at ten and doesn't come back on till eight. Soap and brush are
in the room."

"Thank you."

"What's a good place to eat in town?" asked Bert. He
glanced about the deserted lobby. Overstuffed chairs, ashtrays

and spittoons, wilting potted palms. So low was the ceiling, he had instinctively ducked when they entered.

"Morning Glory Cafe. Only place. Don't order the flapjacks, they're harder than stove lids. And keep clear of the bacon." He leaned close and lowered his voice. "Folks claim Lafe Waterbury sneaks coyote innards in with the real thing. I wouldn't know, I eat to home. You want to leave a wakeup call?"

"I guess," said Bert. He turned to Ben. "What's a good time?" He turned back to the clerk. "What time those two come in before us ask for?"

He checked the column alongside Littlejohn's and Olcott's signature.

"Twelve noon. They plan to catch the twelve-fifty-two train."

"Noon it is. No sense makin' the day man climb the stairs twice."

The clerk stuck the tip of his tongue into the space previously occupied by an incisor, mulled this over, and nodded. He handed Ben the key.

"Dollar and a half, please. In advance."

Ben paid.

"Towels in the room. You'll find two buckets out back. Like I said, the plunge bath's in the hall closet. It's new, try not to dent it, please. A beauty: six feet of heavy tine, a wooden bottom and handles at each end. Japanned blue inside. Smart looking. Sleep well, gents."

The room was discouragingly small. There was barely ten inches of space between the two narrow beds. When Ben set the tub at the foot of his, they had to sidle around it to get at the washstand positioned against the wall opposite the door.

"I been in bigger stagecoaches, for Godsakes," said Bert.

"We can stand it for one night."

Bert undressed and lay down while Ben brought water up. He filled the tub two-thirds full.

"Don't you think you were a little obvious, asking what time they wanted their wake-up call?"

"That's not bein' obvious. That's shrewd. You think he cares I ask about them? He doesn' know 'em from Adam's off ox. Foun' out what we wanted to know, didn' I? An' then some. The twelve-fifty-two train..."

"Where to, I wonder?"

"Who cares, we'll be ridin' right with 'em. Get up at noon, arrange for the horses, buy me some lead for this piece Butz give me. Board the train, keep outta' their sight..."

"Something is beginning to smell funny, Bert."

"Open the window."

"Seriously. The whole chase. Do you ever get the feeling they *want* us to keep on their tail?"

His father eyed him as if he thought he'd suddenly lost his reason.

"They want to get away's what they want."

"I'm beginning to wonder. Go back to the beginning."

Ben sat in the tub scrubbing Kansas from his hide. Bringing a deep, healthy glow to the surface. "Back to Gypsum. You had them locked up. Then you come down with appendicitis. You were down a little more than one day. In the meantime Marshal Butz lets them go. In the time you were out of commission, they could have been across Kansas well into Colorado. Instead, they leave town, then turn around and come back. Why?"

"They changed their minds about somethin'. Maybe about where to stash the Dragon's Eye."

"Maybe. You spot them, chase them, you've got them practically by the coattails when the Stonecifers grab you."

"Ugly trash!"

"You're on the verge of being married when two men show up and begin blasting away. One looks like Littlejohn."

"He had his ears, all right, but all I could see was silhouette 'gainst the sun. Just the shape. Coulda' been anybody."

"You said his ears exactly, that was the word you used. Ears exactly like his. So much so they reminded you of him. Think about this; what if they happened to see the Stonecifers waylay you? Followed all of you to the soddy, waited to see what was going on, and when the minister showed up decided to move in.

"*Decided to raise enough of a ruckus so you could get away.* What if?"

"That makes no sense."

"Let me go on. Hand me the brush, please. Man, this feels good. Okay, you get away from the family, you get back on their tail, but it's been too long. There's no sign of them in Sand City. You and I meet. With nothing to go on, not a clue, we go back to Gypsum to touch bases with Butz. Crowley and Hubbard show up. We run out on them, go to the saloon, and out of the blue, who shows up? Tweedledee and Tweedledum."

"Who?"

"Bert, why would they come back to Gypsum a second time?"

"I already said. They coulda' changed their minds about where to stash the Dragon's Eye."

"Nonsense. If they came back three more times you'd say the same thing."

"How do you know what I'd say? I don' even know myself till I say it."

"Let me finish."

"Well, shake it up. I need a bath as much as you. I'm beat to boots. Oh, I *feel* great, hunnert percent, but tired. You know, battle fatigue."

"They register. They leave a wake-up time. That's not enough, they even tell the clerk what train they're catching."

"Idle, frien'ly conversation. What's so earthshatterin' about that?"

"Idle, friendly conversation. I wonder . . ."

"I wonder, I wonder."

Ben shook his head. "It's almost like *you* were carrying the ruby and *they*'re trying to keep up with you. God forbid they lose you . . ."

"Go through my pockets. You find the Dragon's Eye, I'll eat it."

"I just don't understand it."

"Whyn'cha admit that in the firs' place? Get outta' there."

Ben dumped his bathwater out the window; it spooked a

sleeping cat in the alley below; it screeched in protest. He poured the remaining water into the tub.

"Put it all in, for Godsakes, I'm jus' as dirty as you!"

"No. You don't want to get your incision wet."

Bert had removed the dressing; Ben examined the cut. All eight stitches had either loosened or were broken. There was no bleeding, but the incision looked raw, angry.

"I hope it's not infected. How does it feel?"

"Sore, whatta you think? It's okay. I'm healin'. I got the constitution of an ox."

"You should have a doctor look at it before we leave tomorrow. Get yourself a new set of stitches. You've certainly done a job on the old ones."

"The heck with that. Leave it alone, it'll heal perfect."

"Try not to get it wet."

"Hand me the brush."

● ● ● ●

Bert bought a box of shells for the Classic Peacemaker given him by Marshal Butz. And finally got around to cleaning the seven-and-a-half-inch barrel. He announced it was as gritty as a laying hen's gizzard.

Like Sand City, Ophir Junction offered no station, only the bare platform. Few people waited for the train. Bert and Ben waited across the street in the shadows of the doorway to Peabody's General Merchandise Mart. They stood surrounded by washtubs, wicker baskets, and other household paraphernalia.

The train came in fifteen minutes before the hour. It shuddered noisily to a stop; the engine whooshed steam and puffed a sooty cloud from its straight, round stack. It boasted four pair of driving wheels and looked to have enough power to drag the seven-car string over the Rockies and the Sierra.

"Once upon a time," said Bert, eyeing it skeptically.

"It's got to be at least thirty years old. Kept stuck together with Glidden wire an' hoof glue, you betcha. Look at the rattle on that front drivin' wheel crank, it's 'bout to drop off clean. An' look at the bottom o' the main reservoir there, jus' above the secon' drivin' wheel, it's been patched, for Godsakes.''

"You an authority on locomotives, too?"

"I got eyes. Hey, look who's comin'. . . Look at those ears on Littlejohn. Sun shines right through 'em. If I had ears like that I'd sew 'em to the sides o' my head. Train 'em like they do kids' teeth with braces an' such. I'll betcha a good stiff wind'd pick him right up off'n the ground."

"Let's go."

Bert stayed him. "No rush. Better we mosey on down the street, cross over, an' come up on the las' car from behind. They'll be lookin' out the window, you know."

"Why should they bother? They know we're here. Know we're getting on."

"You still stuck with that tomfool idea?"

"It makes sense, Bert."

A woman wearing an outrageous hat—yards of scarlet cloth wound about and topped with an enormous bird—was coming toward them. They stepped back to let her pass between. Bert tipped his hat and blowed slightly.

"Mornin' . . ."

She appraised him with worried eyes. As if he'd startled her out of a daydream. Without a word, she passed on into the store.

"Frien'ly cuss. Frien'ly town. Let's go."

The train was bound for Russell, Hays, Wakeeny, and Sharon Springs. Then it crossed over into Colorado. Its ultimate final destination was San Francisco, nearly four days away.

"This could set us back a bundle," said Bert. He settled back in his seat, the last seat in the last passenger car in front of the mail car. "How much you figure?"

"Through to San Francisco? A hundred twenty-five at least."

"I ain' got but forty dollars. How much you got?"

"It doesn't matter. It's the U.P. We should be able to wangle a company courtesy break. Let me do the talking. You realize, of course, they may not be going as far as San Francisco. They could get off the first stop."

"Horsemanure. They won't get off till Frisco guaranteed. Bet your life an' your best hat on it."

"Let me handle the conductor. Please."

"I won' say a word."

The engine coughed and choked and sent a tremor down the train. It shook the straw hat off the man seated in front of Ben. He picked it up for him. Ophir Junction passed slowly out of sight through the water-stained window. Bert tilted his hat over his face and snored softly into it.

Ben smiled and settled himself more comfortably. As comfortably as he could, considering the unyielding hardness of the wooden seat. The car was only half-filled. Four seats up sat a drummer, his oversized sample case alongside him. He was regaling two fellow passengers who had turned their seat to face his. A mile out of town, the conductor appeared at the far end. His punch glistened in his hand. He checked seat stubs and paused to sell and punch tickets. Up the aisle he came.

"Tickets. tickets, please..."

Ben showed his Wells Fargo I.D. card. The company's courtesy agreement with the Union Pacfiic had lapsed about the time Lloyd Tevis had taken over from William Fargo as president. A new contract was pending, but the specifics had yet to be agreed on.

He cleared his throat. "My partner here and I are on a case," he said. "The men we're following are up ahead of the second car back of the tender."

"How far you going?"

"It depends on them. We have to keep them in our sights. Possibly clear through to San Francisco."

"That'll be a hundred and twelve dollars each."

"Didn' you hear him?" Bert raised his hat, unmuffling his voice. "He jus' tol' you we're on a case. For the U.P. This *is* a U.P. train, isn' it?"

"Yes, but..."

"You do know about the courtesy agreement between your president, Mr. Jay Gould, and Mr. Bill Fargo, president o' Wells Fargo and Company. Which agreement says that when Wells Fargo detectives such as us are actually workin' on cases involvin' goods or funds stolen from the line, they are to be extended very courtesy up to an' includin' travel. You do know about that.''

"I. . . ."

"I myself had the honor o' bein' in our new president, President Lloyd Tevis's office in the Wells Fargo buildin' on Sansone Street near Halleck in San Francisco when Mr. Gould come to call an' re'firm with President Tevis the agreement first made by Bill Fargo. Your Mr. Gould's quite a stogie smoker, isn' he? Musta' smoked half a dozen down to the butt in that meetin'. It sure was some thrill for a meat-an'-potato man like myself to be invited to sit in on a high-level meetin' between two great presidents o' two great companies like the U.P. an' Wells Fargo. The reason I was invited was 'cause at the time my partner here an' I had just finished cleanin' up the famous Big Springs, Nebraska U.P. express car robbery; you remember, that was the one that made all the papers, where Sam Bass an' five others robbed sixty thousand', which we got back every penny, an' collared all six. Mr. Gould sure was pleased as punch 'bout that one. Insisted I be there personally when he an' Mr. Tevis renewed the agreement.''

"All right, all right . . .''

"I'd 'preciate knowin' your name so we could contact your super an' tell him how you cooperated on this important case.''

"My name's James Fallon, that's two 'lls'. Superintendent Ogilvy in the Omaha office.''

"You got a middle initial?''

"B. James B. Fallon.''

"James B. Fallon an' Superintendent Ogilvy. Got it.''

He restored his hat to his face. The conductor seemed suddenly almost jovial. He punched two tickets and handed Ben their fare paid stubs. And went on his way whistling.

"You should be peddling snake oil off the back of a wagon.''

"It worked, didn' it? A little gentle arm bendin' never hurt anybody.''

He resumed snoring.

Thirty-six hours and many stops later, they passed through Denver. They picked up a second engine to assist in the tortuous climb ahead. In the midst of the ascent, they ran into heavy rains. They climbed over the Rockies, snaking slowly and carefully through the peaks, around treacherous turns bottomed by yawning abysses, and through cuts so narrow one could reach out and touch the sheer walls on either side. They conquered the Vasquez Mountains; they cut through Ute Pass and crossed the Williams River. And headed down the zigzag toward the Utah border.

Bert's estimate of the engine leaped to Ben's mind with every shudder and shake. The helper engine looked only a year or two younger.

The sun rose on the morning of the third day. The first sight to meet Ben's eyes was a sheer drop into hell. He gasped; he clamped his eyes shut and choked down a great lump of terror. Up the vertical defiles climbed pine, juniper, and Douglas fir. Higher still, great stretches of aspen, Lodgepole pine, spruce, and alpine fire took over. But it was the unseeable bottom plunging straight down from the edge of the unseen railbed that seized Ben's heart with the fist of fear and set his brow glistening with cold sweat. His knuckles took on the color of ivory, so tightly did he grip the edge of his seat. He breathed in short gasps; he slowly opened his eyes, only to snap them shut and swallow so hard it hurt.

Bert woke beside him. He glanced at him, looked out the window, and smiled grandly.

"What a great view! Be-yoooo-tiful!"

Ben turned from sight of it and pretended to go back to sleep.

Eight

Early evening of the third day. They had dispensed with the extra, helper engine in Grand Junction just before the Utah border. They crossed over and resumed climbing into the mountains. To Ben these appeared as lofty as those through which they had passed. Why they had dropped the helper engine with so many arduous climbs still to come he could not understand.

"There's no figgerin' how railroad people figger," said Bert.

His last words. Back to sleep he went. Oblivious to the heights to come and to the toll they would take on every passenger's nervous system. Save his.

Like the spine of a gigantic prehistoric creature, the Wasatch Mountains rise in central Utah. They run north to south, carving canyons and ravines down their heavily wooded slopes. Duplicating in depth and frightening beauty those in the Rockies. The rain they had picked up in Denver did not stop until Grand Junction. Then it resumed. It started slowly out of leaden skies, hastening the onset of darkness, slashing against the windows. Lightning streaked the heavens; thunder muttered over the creaking, clacking, and rumble of the train. A vicious cloudburst struck. The wind rose bending the legions of pines like a wheat field. Brooks filled, swelling, overleaping their banks, crashing and careening down the slopes. Joining streams, setting them thrashing, roaring over the rocks. In the fading light of day, Ben could see white water leaping and smashing below. The train had slowed to a crawl in negotiating a narrow bridge of rock around a peak set equidistant between two loftier peaks. Thirty feet below, the running waters joined to fill a stream. It ran ahead on a fairly level plane for nearly half a mile before plunging downward.

The train was barely moving. Out of a curve it came; the yellow light discovered a wooden bridge ahead. It stretched ninety-six feet across a chasm cut at right angles to it. Down the chasm, turbulent, dark waters plummeted, feeding the larger stream running parallel to the tracks.

The train stopped just before the bridge. The passengers jumped from their seats; they crowded the vestibules and flattened their faces against the windows to see what was going on. The fireman and brakeman got down. Lanterns in hand, their slickers shining, they walked on the bridge. They began to inspect it.

It was nearly seven years old but solidly constructed. Extra oak supports a foot square propped up the left side. Some of the sleepers were rotted, but the bridge itself was well engineered. Built to meet the requirements of its unusual position in good weather and poor, it appeared safe from one end to the other.

The men continued their inspection. Though neither was able to climb down underneath on the left side to examine the supporting piers. It was much too steep. A man would have to be let down by rope and suspended just above the roiling waters. Then walk across the sheer face of the rock.

They climbed back up into the cab. They talked briefly with the engineer. Not one but two trains had crossed the Elgin Gorge bridge—for that was its name—earlier that day. The weather had been clear to be sure, the waters normal. But throughout the seven years of its service, the bridge had stood fast, even submerged under spring runoffs of melting snows and flash floods much more powerful than the waters now.

They would go on. The passengers were requested to return to their seats. The eighty-ton locomotive was fired, the throttle lever eased slowly back. The cowcatcher inched forward. The first pair of truck wheels followed. The second. The front driving wheels.

"Some rain," said Bert.

Ben said nothing. He was too busy fighting back his fear, forcing it down his throat into the pit of his stomach where it solidified into a stone. Now the engine was three-quarters onto the bridge. Now all but the trailing truck wheels and cab were on. The trestle creaked with the weight of 160,000 pounds. Onto it rolled the tender followed by the first car, pushing the engine well past the center of the bridge. Down tumbled the swollen waters from above. Suddenly, an immense, dark shape broke the dimly visible skyline overhead. No crew member, not one passenger spied it. All eyes were directed straight ahead. The engineer and fireman stared at the far end of the bridge and the rails beyond supported by solid rock. They beckoned.

Down tumbled the dark shape. It twisted and turned as it came. A split second before it crashed into the trestle, it assumed recognizable form. By calamitous timing, a wagon-road bridge spanning the same water nearly an eighth of a mile above had torn loose and been set hurtling down. It smashed into the trestle full force. Shattered it. Knocked the piers from under it. Sent the engine and tender plunging into the lower stream. Dragging the front half of the train with them.

The world dropped from under Ben and Bert. Up from their seats they shot, heads thumping the ceiling.

Nine

Bert woke. His head rang, his incision stung. The cartilage in his neck felt as if it had snapped. He tested it; he rocked his head gently. His neck was still in one piece. The car lay on its side on the slope; the forward coupling had snapped free. The car ahead had slid down into the water, one side rising above the level. Men bellowed, moaned, and cursed. Women shrieked. Cries of pain filled the darkened car. Bert got to his feet. He stood on the wall under the window out which he had been peering just before the wagon-road bridge struck. He squinted into the darkness of the car.

"Ben . . . Son . . ."

No answer. He felt about; he called again and again. He started toward the rear; his boot smashed the window underfoot. He pulled back; he skirted it, making his way over the seat and slowly, unsteadily up the incline to the door. The car's smashing into the car in front of it in falling had wrenched open the door. It swung easily at his touch. He climbed through. He could hear the groaning and cries of the injured in a melancholy chorus lifiting to the darkened heavens. The rain continued beating down. How many had been killed?, he wondered. Bull's-eye lanterns hovered above. Three cars and the caboose still stood on the approach to the trestle. The engine lay on its side in the swiftly moving stream; the tender was still coupled to it. He saw no sign of either the engineer or fireman. The wagon-road bridge sat squarely in the center of the wrecked trestle. It looked like the piled fuel of an immense bonfire-to-be. Rails twisted like ribbons sprung from their sleepers lay about.

• • • •

Ben had come to before his father. He had tried to rouse him, but could not. He examined Bert, straining to see through the darkness. He didn't seem hurt. He climbed out of the car the same way Bert was to leave moments later. His right shoulder ached furiously; if it wasn't fractured it might as well be, he thought, so badly was it wrenched. He tried to lift his arm; pain stabbed his shoulder. He rubbed it lightly; it restored the circulation and numbed the pain.

He came upon an hysterical elderly woman. He spoke soothingly to her and managed to calm her. Her forehead was cut, but it didn't appear deep. But she was bleeding badly. He bandaged it with a strip torn from the hem of her dress.

He pulled two people from the stream. The second was a heavyset young man and the effort nearly dislocated his aching shoulder. By the time he got him up on the bank, the man was dead. He came upon the fireman; he looked half-mad, his eyes huge and glazed with shock; the rain splattered his face.

"Wasn' nothin' wrong with the tracks or the trestle." He shook his head and addressed the air. "Me an' Roy checked every foot both sides. Water was gettin' fiercer an' fiercer, though. We told Arthur, but he said we should go ahead an' cross before it got any worse. Before the water got up so high it'd bust 'gainst the side an' swirl up, an' wash over the rails. That's what he said . . ."

He babbled on, lapsing into incoherence. There was nothing Ben could do for him. For the rest of his days he would live with the horror of this night and his part in it. Wouldn't they all! He looked upward through the glistening curtain of rain at the ruined trestle and its burden. He looked at the survivors, the injured, the dead. What a weak, helpless, thoroughly pitiful creature man is, he thought; how fragile his destiny; how uncertain his lot in the game of chance that life is.

Someone ran back along the tracks to the station at Gilroy, a little mining town through which they had passed. The telegraph operator there sent the stunning news ahead to the upcoming station, and to Provo and Salt Lake City. A relief train was sent out. The rain, meanwhile, had slackened. It finally stopped entirely; the streams refused to subside. They seemed to glory in their suddenly discovered ability to destroy, kill, and maim.

The dazed fireman continued to stumble about looking for the engineer. He didn't seem to realize that he alone had been able to jump clear of the cab before the engine hit the water.

Bert came across Ben ministering to an old man.

"He's badly hurt," said Ben, his expression at sight of his father unchanging.

"He's dead, son. Look at the back of his head, it's all stove in."

In the days to come, the whole story of that dreadful night would establish that sixty-eight people were killed instantly or died soon after the crash. Twenty-three drowned. Twenty-one bodies were recovered; some carried as far away as six miles downstream. Help finally arrived, coming from Gilroy and Eldorado, four miles further on. The injured, the dead, and the survivors were carried in wagons to Eldorado. Bert's and Ben's horses had been riding in the baggage car with other passengers' mounts. The car had never left the tracks; they were unhurt. The Slaughters rode into Eldorado. They followed the last wagon carrying, among others, Frank Littlejohn. His partner, Olcott, was nowhere to be seen.

"Prob'ly washed downstream," said Bert. "With the Dragon's Eye in his pocket. Wouldn' you know . . ."

"Don't complain. We could have drowned just as easily. Littlejohn, too. Olcott could be in one of the wagon's up ahead."

"I doubt it. Not with our luck. Whatta mess. Tradegy on a gran' scale, that's what the newspaper'll be callin' this night."

"Tragedy."

"That's what I said. As if things weren't bad enough I've gone an' lost bettern' half o' plug o' Battle Ax..."

• • • •

Morning arrived, clear, mild, and beautiful in tiny Eldorado. The injured had been brought to the local schoolhouse; it had been hastily converted into an aid station. Bert, Ben, and the others were put up in a partially filled warehouse at the local lumberyard. Given cots, blankets, and coffee by a group of energetic ladies. Father and son found a private corner behind an eight-foot-high stack of two-by-fours. It served to keep them out of Littlejohn's sight.

Olcott turned up with his left wrist heavily bandaged and in a sling. A large square of court plaster was affixed to his forehead. Bert spotted him when he woke up. He was the first one awake. He went to check on their horses. When he came back he woke Ben; the others were getting up. The ladies who had come to their aid the night before were serving hot breakfast.

"I checked at the stable," said Bert. "Our two friends got no horses. They musta' sold 'em before they boarded the train. Likely figgered they'd be ridin' clear through to Frisco or wherever they're headin'."

"What'll they do now?"

"Take a stage down outta' these hills to Salt Lake City. Catch a train there." He grinned. "Any stage leavin' here'll be packed to the racks. They'll charge a hunnert bucks a head for fifteen inches o' space. Serves those two right, the thievin' scum."

• • • •

They stood in shadow inside the stable door. The local stage line was not Wells Fargo, Ben noticed. High up in the Rockies, the Wasatch Mountains and other ranges small independent lines served the little towns. This one was the McLemore Overland Transportation Company. It was Provo-bound.

"Cross your fingers it won't be too full they can't get on," said Bert.

The passengers were assembling in front of the office door. A man in vest and shirt sleeves bustled about, clipboard in hand. Bert and Ben watched and waited. A McLemore overland stage came trundling up at seven-thirty on the dot. Passengers piled aboard. Littlejohn and Olcott were among them.

"SAN FRANCISCO, HERE WE COME!" said Bert.

"Keep it down. Why must you always draw attention to yourself?"

Father looked son up and down, his expression as sour as he could make it. "I'm pretty. Folks enjoy lookin' at me. Shut up."

They let the stage get five minutes away; they mounted up and started out.

• • • •

Lloyd Tevis was unused to heat directed at him from high places. Never before in his life had he felt it. His rung on the ladder of achievement was so high, whenever pressure threatened he would refocus it upon his subordinate officers. But when the federal Government in the persons of the president, the secretary of state, and the ambassadors to and from Belgium focused their heat upon him, there was no one he could divert it to. It burned with such savage intensity he felt as if he'd been dipped into a cauldron of burning oil.

He could and did revile the Slaughters in absentia; he also vented his frustration on Chief Hume and Superintendent John Valentine. But in Washington's eyes it was Tevis and no one else who must answer for his company's failure to recover the Dragon's Eye. When Mace Crowley and Wardell Hubbard wired Hume, telling him that the Slaughters had skipped out on them, it was the last straw. Into Hume's office Tevis stormed, battle flags flying. His appearance stunned the chief. In his sixty-one years of life Hume had seen many an irate man, but in his wildest nightmare he could never envision the state of wrath into which Tevis had pitched himself. His normally pallid face approached the color of raw liver. Fire shot from his eyes; he spoke through jaws clenched so tightly his teeth threatened to shatter; his voice resembled a dull saw cutting through steel. He shook all over; he looked to be on the verge of bursting a blood vessel. When Hume politely gestured him to a chair, he snatched it up and made as if to hurl it through the window. The chief stopped him just in time.

"WE'RE FINISHED! DONE!"

"Take it easy, take it easy . . ."

"The president is furious! Livid! Everyone in Washington is throwing knives at us. The newspapers are crucifying us! Thank God Belgium is only an overgrown duchy. If this were England, France, or Germany, they'd declare war!"

"Calm down, sir, you'll have a heart attack . . ."

"I WANT ONE! A stroke, anything to lay me low. I'd welcome a coma. I can't eat, can't sleep. I've lain awake the last four nights staring into space, seeing that damnable ruby big as your fist staring back at me like some loathsome nightmare creature's eye. Burning into my brain! The gall of those two; they not only refuse to contact us—when we send men in to help them, they run out on them! Of all the unmitigated brass!"

Back and forth he stomped before the twin windows overlooking the bay, hands clasped behind his back, neck veins swelling, protruding, threatening to burst their flesh. His face darkened by the second; his fury seemed to squeeze his windpipe, forcing him to gasp and gulp for breath.

"They'll pay in blood for this. Firing's too good for 'em. We'll press charges. I'll see them behind bars. They'll get twenty years. SO HELP ME GOD THEY WILL!"

It took Hume nearly fifteen minutes to quiet him. He finally got him into a chair. His voice came down an octave, his cheeks lightened from purple to rose. Hume made no attempt to defend the Slaughters. Had he even mentioned their names, Tevis would have attacked him with the chair. The situation had battered his pride; in his mind, the company's reputation had been utterly destroyed. Everything he had worked for, the fruits of nearly eleven years of effort in building Wells Fargo into the most successful and renowned express-banking firm in the world, had been wrested from him with the theft of a precious stone he had never even seen. Spurring his suffering was the Slaughters' gall, their shameless impudence in willfully ignoring his explicit command to contact their chief.

"If I ever see either of them face to face again I'll strangle them. SO HELP ME GOD I WILL! They dare show themselves around here ever again, I'll kill them if I hang for it!"

Hume sighed silently. He was by nature an easygoing sort. Rarely given to temperamental outbursts; a man who required little to imbue him with peace and contentment. Give him his favorite Cuban cigar, his rose garden, his collection of scenic views of San Francisco and the Bay Area, and his stereoscope with its polished cherrywood frame, give him his cat Eloise, his bachelorhood, and a decently cooked meal and he was happy. Unlike Tevis, he was no slave to ambition, no glutton for power. He had seen the elephant. For all his brilliant business mind, iron gut, impenetrable skin, and armor of arrogance, Tevis had yet to.

In his job, Hume was able and efficient, astute and skilled in dealing with others. Prior to joining Wells Fargo he had been marshal of Placerville, California. Before that he was sheriff of El Dorado County. At one time he had been warden of the state prison in Carson City.

He respected but did not admire Tevis; did not especially like the man. But he sympathized with him in the present situation. He also sympathized with the Slaughters. Unlike Tevis, he was able to view the problem through the lens of realism unclouded by emotion. He recognized that father and son operated somewhat like mavericks. Bert in particular rarely bothered to inform the home office when at work on a case. And broke any rule in the book when he felt like it. But both got results and more consistently than did any team that followed the letter of the rules. Their record of cases solved was outstanding, the best in the company. Hume had no doubts but that they were on top of the case. And in due time would report their success in breaking it. They'd recover the ruby; they'd bring in the culprits.

Neither he nor anyone under his command could control the actions of the men in the field. They were on their own. If the Slaughters saw fit to run out on Crowley and Hubbard, they must have their reasons. Whatever was going on, he saw no reason to shelve his faith in Egbert and Benjamin.

And whatever the outcome, he would stick by them. When it was over, if Tevis fired them, he would have to seriously consider tendering his resignation. This decided, he continued nodding mechanically at Tevis's threats and pronouncements. He got out a Chicos, lit it, and managed to reduce it by half to a fine ash by the time his visitor gave up ranting and left.

"Good luck, Egbert, Benjamin." He watched the door ease partially closed behind Tevis.

To the devil with President Grant. To hell with Secretary of State Fish and both ambassadors. Grant was no hero to him anyway; he'd voted for his Democratic opponent, Horatio Seymour.

Ten

Provo huddled at the base of the precipitous Wasatch Range. Its western face rose nearly perpendicular. To the north, the long bulk of Mount Timpanagas towered more than 12,000 feet. The overloaded stage picked its precarious way slowly down the narrow, zigzagging road riding the brake hard. Heating it almost to charring.

The scenery was magnificent. The Wasatch was formed of Archeozoic rocks a billion, 850-million-years old. The oldest formations in the world. Squat, full, scaly-barked willow, irregularly crowned red birch, slender, quaking aspen that lifted to a hundred feet, and cottonwood rose to meet the fir and pine forest commanding the higher elevations. Dense thickets of rail-straight maple, gnarled and rugged-looking scrub oak, bushy chokecherry, and mountain mahogany crowded the lower slopes. Indian paintbrush waved delicately in the breeze, legions of dogtooth violets flaunted their bright yellow blossoms, trumpet-shaped flowers of slender-stalked blue and red penstema, grape-purple clusters of monkhood, pretty, pink mallow bells and dozens of other wildflowers spread bright splotches of color amidst the sweeping patterns of mingled shades of green.

The stage reached ground level; it ran a mile more, then halted at the first stop. There the leg-weary team would be replaced with fresh horses. Five miles beyond, Provo occupied a wide terrace of prehistoric Lake Bonneville along the south bank of the Provo River. Like other Mormon-built towns, it was crisscrossed with wide streets laid out in the four cardinal points of the compass. Houses sat well back on spacious green lawns. Backyards boasted vegetable and flower gardens. Shade trees were liberally scattered about town: Lombardy and Caroline poplars, black-barked Norway maples, and box elder strewing its brittle branches about the ground.

Bert and Ben pulled their weary horses up about a mile east of the stage stop. Bert nodded toward it.

"They'll switch over to the U.P. in Provo, watch. Everybody on board will. They've had their bellies fulla' stagin' by now."

Ben dismounted. He drank from his canteen. He poured water into his hat to give his mount. The sun was unusually bright, hanging in the glaring sky as white as glossy paper. It withered the parched vegetation and hazed the horizon. Above it, an armada of fat, white ghost riders drifted southward. From a distance they could see the driver motioning his passengers back into the stage. It rolled away. The Slaughters followed; they kept their distance. The stage soon disappeared around a large outcropping, a ledge as high as a barn through which the road had been cut. Ben pulled up.

"What are you stoppin' for?"

He had gotten down. He examined his horse's left forehoof. "Look at this . . ."

A single nail was all that held the shoe on. Bert held the horse's leg between his knees; Ben pulled off the shoe and put it in his saddlebag. They were preparing to go on when they suddenly heard a flurry of shots ahead. They resembled the light tapping of sticks against a drumhead.

"What in hell . . ."

Both broke into a gallop; they rounded the turn and spied a holdup in progress. They backed off not of sight, dismounted, and flattened to look. Men with rifles stood high up on rocks on both sides of the road. Three of them were relieving the passengers of their valuables. The shotgun messenger's Winchester lay where he had tossed it. He and the driver stood on their box, hands upraised. Bert squinted, blinked, and gasped. "LOOK!"

The man in charge had removed his hat and was holding it out to a young, well-dressed woman. She dropped first her bracelet, then her ring into it. His greasy black hair gleamed in the sunlight; it was long, stringy, and hung to his shoulders. He was thin, rangy-looking, built like a thousand others Bert had met down the years: sinew and bones. But for one distinct difference.

He had only one eye. With his hat off, Bert could clearly see the hideous scar with the hole in its center where his right eye should have been. It was his badge, God's down payment demanded of him for the savagery and heartache he wreaked on decent, innocent people. One day he would be killed and go to hell and there pay in full for his sins. Bert was as certain of this as he was that the ground was beneath his feet. One-eye would die kicking and in excruciating pain by his hands: gun, knife, whatever. This would come to pass. It was foreordained.

"Rance Cutler," said Ben.

"Praise the Lord."

Bert mounted, drew, and urged his horse forward. Ben nearly pulled him from his saddle, catching his arm.

"Leggo!"

"Stay where you are. See for yourself, he's got them cold. But nobody's been hurt, not yet. You go barreling in and somebody might be. Look at the firepower he's got on both sides. What do you think—they'll close their eyes, let you ride in and hit him?"

"He's not gettin' away this time . . ."

"He won't, only let's do it right."

"Like you did down to Arizona that time, when you had him cold an' let him off the hook?"

Ben had mounted while he was talking. He reached down and grabbed Bert's reins. He wheeled both horses about and trotted a few yards further back.

"The last thing we need is a shootout. Somebody's bound to get hurt." He softened his tone. "I know how you feel . : ."

"YOU DON'T! You never have. The motherless dung heap killed your mother! Shot her down defenseless on the Cedar City road. Rode away, left her dead in the dust. Murderin' scum! BASTARD! LEGGO MY HORSE!"

"Take it easy . . ."

"LEGGO!"

He snarled viciously; he snatched back his reins and swung about. Ben bolted up alongside.

"Don't be a fool!"

Bert backhanded him; hard. His expression suddenly pure hatred. Ben shook it off.

"Bert, please. You'll only get innocent people killed. Is that what you want? Would mother? Listen to me, they're almost finished with them. They'll let them go on their way. You follow, keep on Littlejohn's and Olcott's tails. I'll follow Cutler . . ."

"Like hell. He's mine. If I got to kill everybody 'round him to get to him. He's not gettin' away, not this time . . ."

"Of all the freakish things to happen."

Bert started. "What are you sayin'? You dis'pointed we come on him? Great God, it's what I've prayed for! What ails you, don'tcha have any heart, any guts? Dont'cha have the guts to take the bull by the horns when it runs up into your face? What are you, some kinda' milksop?"

"Cut it out. I at least keep my head, I don't go hog-wild."

"You don' do nothin', that's your trouble!"

Hooves pounded. Bert cursed and lurched off. Again Ben grabbed his reins. Pulled up short, Bert's horse stumbled, its head twisting about at an awkward angle, nearly ripping the bit from its mouth. Again Bert swore and swung, smashing Ben on the side of the head, tumbling him hard into the road.

Ben did not lose consciousness. The scenery swam, a loud gong resounded; Bert's fleeing figure softened and melted into his dust. He shook off the pain, the dizziness. He scrambled up.

"BERRRRRRRRRT!"

If Bert heard he made no sign. Doubled low in his saddle he was into the chase. Heading south toward Thistle. The lowering sun brightened his right shoulder. Far ahead of him, the dust of Cutler and his seven men merged, forming a single, huge, dun-colored cloud.

* * * *

Ben got to the Provo train station just in time to catch sight of Frank Littlejohn boarding. He had earlier decided that the two outlaws would ride the train all the way to San Francisco. He had reached Provo and made a deal with the first stableman he came across; his horse and gear he sold for two-thirds of their combined worth.

The station platform was packed; when he boarded, he discovered the train was all but full, with standees in the aisles and vestibules of nearly every car. It looked like the Mormons were making their exodus from the territory. He had to walk to the last car before he found an empty seat.

Worries gathered in his mind as he settled back; he gazed unseeing out the window. Bert was his main concern: his condition, operation, fatigue, his ungovernable temper where Cutler was involved. Mere sight of the snake seemed to strip him of all self-control. His hand went to the side of his head where his father had hit him. His last sight of him before he hit the ground had been Bert's face: as black with fury as he'd every seen it.

Where was he heading? Where would Cutler lead him? Bert would follow him to Guatemala, down to Patagonia if need be. He hoped he wouldn't be so rash, so bullheaded as to try to take the whole crew to get at Cutler. Against such odds he wouldn't stand a chance. If he were smart, he'd use the time it took to catch up to calm himself down. Stay well back and plan his future moves. Wait till they stopped to divide the loot and break up. *If* such was their intention. It was what holdup-types generally did after the job. It forced whoever might be following to scatter.

His second worry was the Dragon's Eye. In the holdup, had Littlejohn and Olcott been forced to turn it over? Did they even have it so they could? Good questions. Yet it was hard to believe that they'd go through all they had so far only to hand the stone to highline riders. The poetic justice in it he could see, but no logic.

He still believed they were trying to keep Bert on *their* tails. Not the other way around. Why they should he couldn't fathom, but the suspicion wouldn't go away.

A third worry: San Francisco. End of the trail. In his gut he felt that that would be where it all would wind up. In Wells Fargo's backyard with the cards well stacked against him. With Chief Hume and Lloyd Tevis breathing fire at him. For certain he and Bert had already been fired. Six times over. Which didn't upset him; they could both use a vacation, Bert especially. For the past week he'd been running on adrenalin, wearing himself out and into an early grave.

His shoulder still ached from the train accident. Had Bert's incision started bleeding again? He wondered. If it did, he'd ignore it of course. But what if infection set in?

Willows and cottonwoods sped by; twilight rosied the landscape. Utah Lake stretched as far as he could see, tranquil as a pond. He and the two would have to change over to the Western Pacific come Salt Lake City. His ticket would take him clear through. He dug in his pocket for it. It wasn't there; his fingers flew into one pocket after another; it wasn't anywhere.

"Where the devil . . ."

The conductor came teetering toward him, hand-over-handing the seats.

"Tickets, tickets please . . ."

He seemed to have mislaid it, he explained. The conductor listened politely, pursing his liver-colored lips.

"It was the paid-for stub."

He displayed his I.D. He began piling it on as Bert had done. His father's every selling point he repeated almost word for word. But listening to himself he could feel none of the conviction Bert so ably injected in his speech. He had been positively glib. That this conductor had eyes as icy as Lloyd Tevis's and a jaw as formidable looking as a granite wall did not help. He sensed he was floundering.

"Wells Fargo and the Union Pacific have had an arrangement between them for years, as you know."

He was trying his utmost to sound casual. He almost added one hand washes the other; he caught himself just in time. Such a sleazy phrase...

His listener bunched his mouth and crinkled his brow. "What you want is a free ride, right?"

"I... wouldn't put it that way."

"What way would you put it?"

"All I'm saying is that Wells Fargo has an agreement with the U.P., with all the major lines."

"Never heard of it. Course, I only been in this job nine years. Plenty goes on I don't know about. I know we got an arrangement with the Pinkertons." He winked and grinned. "You wouldn't be trying to diddle an old man, would you?"

Ben flushed. He ran his finger around his neck inside his collar. The conductor raised his hand; stopping further words.

"You do have an honest face, but it's getting pinker by the minute. And you're sweating. And stop running your finger inside your collar like that, you'll tear the button loose.

"Son, I've seen your card, heard your song and dance. I don't believe a word you say, but you're trying so hard I'd have to have a heart of stone to turn you down."

"Thank you..."

"Don't thank me, I'm turning you down. I may hate myself in the morning, but that's the way it goes. San Francisco, did you say? That'll be eighty-nine dollars even. Cash. No checks. And if you're on the level, all you have to do is turn your stub in to get a refund. Eighty-nine dollars, please."

Ben paid. Without another word. The conductor grinned and moved on. The man seated beside Ben had not altered his expression a wrinkle throughout the exchange. He appeared stone-deaf. But Ben doubted it. He slumped lower in his seat. Again his cheeks flushed.

Disgusting, he reflected, the only word to describe it. So disconcerted had Bert had the other conductor, so off-balance, he had gotten him completely flustered. By the time he'd wound it up, the man was practically pleading with him to *take* the ticket from him.

How did he do that?

"Who cares, I don't want to know."

Bert should be ashamed. Gutter tactics.

"Outrageous!"

"Beg your pardon . . ." blurted the man seated beside him.

"Nothing."

• • • •

2

Bert followed Cutler and his gang south into darkness. They did not stop. They didn't even slow until outside Asphalt, just beyond Thistle. Thistle they had skirted. Now they pulled up in a small grove of trees. They divided the loot. There were a couple ill-tempered exchanges and one fairly prolonged argument; then they broke up and went their separate ways. Clouds shrouded the moon and stars. Bert lay in the grass about fifty yards from them; he watched, he listened. When they broke up, he remounted. He isolated Cutler from the rest and followed him south southwest toward Clinton. It lay east of the Payson Forest Reservation.

He picked up speed; he quickly closed the gap between them; soon he was only ten yards behind. The sweet taste of triumph warmed his mouth. His heart swelled. Showdown time coming up!

"You're mine at last, you scum . . ."

No mistaking that broad back and the plainsman's hat set dead level his head, flat as a cake on a counter. He heard Bert's horse behind him; he turned to look back just as the moon came out. Bert had gone to his iron. He aimed, squinted, gaped, and swore.

Cutler pulled up.

Only it wasn't Cutler. Face to face in the moonlight he looked nothing like him. His cheeks were chubby, his mustache neatly clipped; he looked a good ten years older. He had both eyes and displayed a livid scar midway between his chin and mouth. Like Cutler's, his hair was long and black; their builds were somewhat alike, but there the resemblance ended.

Bert glared. "Who the devil are you?"

"What you doin' follyin' me?"

He went for his gun. Bert blew it away. He swore, grabbed his hand, and shook off the pain. Fear drained his cheeks.

"Who are you, mister? What do you want with me?"

"Which way did Cutler head?"

"Who?"

Again Bert fired. Two quick shots, one zipping under each earlobe.

"HEY, CHRISSAKES!"

"Which way?"

"South. Off . . . off to the right a mite . . ."

"Where's he headin'?"

"I dunno. He didn't say, honest . . ."

Bert had moved up close. He lifted his gun. He cocked and aimed squarely at his face. The man swallowed. His upraised hands shook like leaves.

"Where?"

"I dunno! Honest to God in heaven I don't!"

Bert raised a hair. He fired. A hole showed dead center his hat.

"Get goin'. RIDE! You so much as turn aroun' to look back I'll kill you!"

• • • •

Cutler was heading down territory to Arizona. Had to be. Through Arizona, over the border into Mexico. Into the Sierra Occidental. He'd never make it, never get as far as the Arizona line. Bert veered right. The outlaws had stopped in the grove for no more than seven or eight minutes. Just long enough for their horses to catch their breaths. By now Cutler's would have to be as tired as his. He'd have to stop soon. Only where? For how long?

He lifted his gaze and scanned the now brightened heavens. The air was strangely still; very warm but dry. No dampness, no hint of rain. The clouds were shredding. He slowed; he came out of the tall grass back onto the road. It ran straight as fence wire as far as he could see ahead. To his left the darkened bulk of a barn came into view.

"Screw it . . ."

He would sleep and rest his horse. Four hours, not a minute more. Then back on the trail. He'd catch up, when and under what circumstances he had no idea; but he would. Ben could handle Littlejohn, Olcott, and the Dragon's Eye. They'd get back together sooner or later; though probably not till Frisco.

"Firs' things firs', Mr. Tevis, sir. This little set-to's been put off too long as it is. Sixteen years. That's long, wouldn' you say, Mr. Tevis? Sir?"

He sat in a pile of sweet-smelling hay; the horse nibbled at his bed. He had taken off his boots; he wriggled his toes and massaged his feet. His stomach grumbled. He bit off a chaw of Battle Ax: best substitute in the world for food. Hunger he could take; thirst was something else. In the long stretches of sandy wasteland to the south, he would find little or no water. He would have to refill his canteen before much further. Either that or wind up sucking a bullet to slake his thirst. That also served, but not as good as tobacco for hunger.

He lit a match and examined his incision. It was infected. He squeezed pus. It no longer stung, but was sore: like a boil come to its head. He clenched his teeth and held his breath. One by one he picked out the broken stitches. Then he washed it.

He chewed away his hunger, then lay back. His incision he left uncovered to let the air get at it. He prepared to set the clock of his brain for sunup; but before he did so he let his mind drift back to Stockton. That tragic day sixteen years before.

The Wells Fargo depot. He could never forget the date: June 5th; Ben's birthday. His seventh. They had walked to the depot that afternoon to meet Ariel. The stage was due in all the way from Kansas City at four o'clock. She had been gone for ages. How they'd missed her! Seemed like a year and a day . . .

Four o'clock had come. No sign of the stage. Over the wire came explanation for the delay. They had been held up outside of Cedar City. The driver and shotgun messenger had been killed; a passenger, one of three elderly ladies on board, was also dead. So they'd said at first; then changed their minds. It was a young woman that had been killed.

Ariel.

Gunned down by Rance Cutler. His name and the details they'd found out days later. They pieced together what had happened from the other passengers' stories. Cutler had confronted her; he demanded she turn out her bag. Flustered, nervous, she had instead reached into it. He suspected she was going for a gun. He didn't wait to see. He fired.

She had had no gun; she'd never carried one in her life. She feared and detested guns.

He had killed her on Ben's birthday. The happiest day of his year was suddenly the blackest day of his life. Thanks to Cutler. What a blow for a seven-year-old; what a burden for those small shoulders to bear, for that little heart to carry. Never again would he see his mother's smile; never hear the music of her laughter, feel her comforting, loving arms around him, her cheek warm against his. Never again see her across the dinner table, her lovely dark eyes, glistening chestnut hair, her beauty . . .

"Ariel, my darlin', I will always love you. Only you. Me an' Ben. There'll never be another but you. Ariel, Ariel . . ."

He sniffed; he wiped his nose with his sleeve and his eyes with the heels of his hands. He lay back and was soon asleep.

Eleven

Luck comes in streaks. It can avoid one for so long you begin to believe you'll never see it again. Then, when least expected, it shows. It joins you, supports you. You begin to revel in it. Certain that now it's back it will never leave again. Then it vanishes.

Such was Bert Slaughter's experience with luck over the years. He did not catch up with Cutler the day after his night in the barn; nor the day after that. It wasn't until midmorning the third day chasing that his luck swiveled about.

He helped it. He stopped for food and a bottle. He bought oats and water for his horse. Circleville was tiny, neglected, sorry looking. It sat on the south fork of the nearly dried-up Sevier River, just south of Junction. The Paiute County seat.

Nearly thirty miles separated Circleville from Panguitch, the next town of any size. Bert considered this distance; it led him to figure that Cutler had also stopped in Circleville.

But only if he was still heading south, continuing along the same route.

He was. He'd passed through only an hour before. The smelly, self-assured, box-chinned little stableman started nodding halfway through Bert's description.

"I see him. Only when he left he didn' take the Panguitch road." Bert stiffened. The man pointed south a little to the left of the road. "He headed overland toward Mount Dutton. And the Paunscaugant Plateau."

89

"You sure?"

"Said I seen him, didn't I? Couldn't help but notice. Everybody else takes the road."

"Headin' straight down would get him to the Arizona border faster, though."

"Birds seem to think so, though him having no wings, I could see he'll likely want to cut around Ebenezer's Canyon."*

Bert thanked him. He paid him for the fodder and for his brushing down the horse while he himself ate. On he rode. Cutler appeared to be in no grand rush to get to Mexico. *If* that was where he was heading. He was now only an hour behind him. He must have treated himself and his mount to an extra-long night's sleep. It figured. He'd come nearly 200 miles from the scene of the holdup; he'd hardly suspect anyone following would still be at it.

He hoped he'd catch up soon. Have it out, finish him off, close the book for good. His heart was still eager to chase. But the grind, the heat, the long hours in the saddle were beginning to tell. Sleep no longer restored him; the grueling pace should have at least spurred his appetite. It did not. He blamed his incision. The flesh around the stitches had hardened over the past two days. It was inflamed, filled with infection. The tiny stitch holes drained slightly, but not enough to cleanse it and relieve the mounting pressure. It had started to throb and was sore to the touch. He mounted and dismounted and bent and twisted more and more gingerly; he grit his teeth against the expected stab of pain.

What he ought to do was stay in Circleville. Find a doctor and have it tended to. This he couldn't do. Couldn't risk losing Cutler again after working so hard to get this close. One look at his operation and a doctor would probably want to open and drain it. The discomfort he could stand, but the time it would take was too precious to squander.

"Firs' things firs'. Collar the snake, finish him, then see to the friggin' thing."

---

* The local name of a canyon later formally designated as Bryce Canyon. After Ebenezer Bryce, an early settler in the region.

Twelve

Belgian Crown Jewels Exhibition Cancelled
Special from the New York Tribune

Ambassador Roger Van Rooten of Belgium
announced today that the Belgian crown jewels,
which had been on display to the American public
in New York, Chicago, and St. Louis, were being
returned to Antwerp at the behest of the Belgian
royal family. The centerstone of His Majesty King
Leopold's crown, a magnificent ruby weighing 62½
carats, was stolen, and there has been no clue as
to its present whereabouts. The U.S. government
has tendered a formal apology to the royal family.
A spokesman for the Secret Service announced
yesterday that a nationwide effort is now underway
to recover the missing gem. Wells Fargo & Company,
which had been providing security for the collection
during its stay in this country, has been formally
relieved of its duties by the president. A $10,000
reward has been posted for information leading to
the arrest and conviction of the thieves and recovery
of the ruby.

King Leopold Requests Return of Crown Jewels

King Leopold of Belgium has notified President Grant
of his desire for the immediate return of the Belgian
crown jewels, which had been on traveling exhibition
in this country. His Majesty cited the theft of the
ruby centerstone of his crown and his concern over
the safety of the entire collection as the reasons for
his request.

No trace of the stolen ruby has been found. The
team of Wells Fargo detectives assigned to guard
the collection, and who were accompanying it from
St. Louis to San Francisco when the theft took place,
are continuing to investigate, according to a spokesman
for the company.

An Inside Job?

The Wells Fargo detectives assigned to guard the
Belgian crown jewels enroute from St. Louis to San
Francisco have now become the chief suspects in
the theft of the ruby centerstone of King Leopold's
crown.

The company acknowledges that no word has been
received from Detectives Egbert and Benjamin
Slaughter who, with two Belgian Secret Service men,
were entrusted with the safekeeping of the collection
during its stay in this country.

F. Wiley Sunderland, Chief of the U.S. Secret
Service, has informed the president that every effort
is being made to track down the Slaughters in the
belief that their apprehension will lead to recovery
of the missing gem.

So announced *The Desert Evening News, The Salt Lake Tribune,* and *The Salt Lake Herald.* The horror story of the hour
was getting similar treatment in every newspaper in the country,
decided Ben. He folded the *Herald* and dropped it to the floor
of the car on top of the two other papers.

The train had reached Salt Lake City. The conductor had
announced that all passengers changing over to the Western

Pacific must hang onto their paid-for stubs. They would be honored on the ensuing leg to the coast. The train they were to board had yet to be assembled. There would be a forty-minute delay before departure. Thirty minutes had passed. The conductor came through a second time; there would be an additional half-hour delay, "due to minor equipment breakdown." It was at this point that Ben got off the train and bought the three papers.

The last item, the one in the *Herald,* started him steaming. So he and Bert were now prime suspects, were they? For a week now they'd been breaking their necks, chasing all over creation to recover the damned thing, and this was the thanks they got. It was disgusting! Infuriating! But not unexpected. Still, keeping in touch with Hume wouldn't have changed anything. Failure to recover the ruby had to turn the finger of suspicion on them sooner or later. The reporters had to seize on that. He was surprised it had taken them this long.

He thought about Bert and Cutler. He thought about the long, gruelling trek southward; the toll it must be taking on Bert. His incision wasn't healing at all properly: he wasn't helping it; ignoring it wasn't helping, either. It could easily become badly infected. Could peritonitis set in at this stage? *After* removal of his appendix?

Of course. And no doubt had. Once it took hold, it would rage through his flesh. It could kill him in a day. The pace he set for himself, the beating his body was taking, only hastened trouble.

"Damn!"

He should never have let Bert run off after Cutler. Should have spotted his good right hand coming, ducked, and counterpunched. Knocked him cold, draped him over his horse. By the time he came to, Cutler would be miles away. Not that that would discourage Bert from going after him. And when Bert did come around, he'd be so furious he'd probably break *Ben's* neck! There was just no winning with Bert where Cutler was concerned. But he did wish he'd gone along. He'd willingly take all kinds of abuse if he could help protect Bert. And help him finish the job.

His anger was up. He got up and stormed off the train,

muttering, swearing, attracting eyes. Littlejohn and Olcott were as much to blame as Cutler. True, the bad penny had turned up at the worst possible time, but those two had started it all.

He glanced up and down the platform. He saw neither. He went inside the station. Customers crowded the little restaurant counter. He could use a hot cup of coffee, but getting close enough to the counter to order one looked impossible. He spied Littlejohn carrying a cup out of the crowd; he headed back out the door.

The jug-eared little tramp! Where was Olcott, he wondered. Not in the crowd at the counter. If he was, Littlejohn would have waited at the door for him. Instead he'd gone back out. Ben followed. Littlejohn stood by himself at the corner of the building; he sipped his coffee and stared straight ahead. Ben turned and walked briskly around the station. Up behind Littlejohn he came, jammed his gun into the small of his back, and reached around and relieved him of his .45. He shoved it into his belt out of sight under his jacket.

"Don't raise your hands. Don't move if you know what's good for you."

"Dddddon't shoot! I ain't got but eleven bucks. So help me, I'll show you . . ."

"Never mind. Turn around. Keep your hands down I said . . ."

"Yes, ssssssir."

He gaped at Ben.

Ben narrowed his eyes. "Where's your partner?"

"What partner?"

Ben jammed the gun hard into his gut. "Let's cut the clowning. Hand over the ruby. If you ask what ruby, I'll kill you where you stand. I've been itching to ever since Gypsum."

"Please don', please. I ain't well; I gotta weak heart. Doc says one o' the weakest he's ever seed. An' I got no kin . . ."

"The ruby!"

"I ain' got it. Honest. Henry has . . ."

"Let's go find him."

"He's gone."

"What?"

" 'S the God's truth. Honest. We split up in Provo."

"He boarded the train with you. I saw him."

"Maybe you thought you did. You couldn' have. Honest to God. He's gone on to Frisco. He's got the ruby, been carryin' it all along. I don' mind, I just as soon he did. It's gettin' so it scares me. I'm not no perfessional like him an' the others. This is my firs' time. Honest! I been on the straight an' narrow my whole . . ."

"Shut up, I'm not interested. If you're lying . . ."

"I'm not! Check the crowd why don'tcha? Check the train . . . You can look all over town you won' find him. He's gone." He licked his fat lips and gaped foolishly. "Where's your partner?"

"What makes you think I've got one? Never mind. Tell me your plan, chapter and verse, and it better be the truth."

"I dunno the whole of it. Just that Henry's s'posed to go on ahead an' make contact with some fella."

"What 'fella'? What's his name?"

"I dunno, honest! Please stop jabbin' me with that thing; it hurts. I got a stomach ulcer, it pains me something fierce. He's from Australia. Comin' to San Francisco to buy the stone. He figgers he'll sell it back to the king."

He made sense, reflected Ben. Ransoming it would certainly be easier than trying to peddle it on the open market. Or cutting it up.

"How is Olcott carrying it?"

"Got a special pocket inside his pants leg." He indicated on his own. "Fits neat as a pin."

"Okay, this is what we're going to do. You and I will keep going all the way to the end. You'll behave yourself; you won't try anything stupid. You won't try to get away. If you do, when I catch up I'll kill you. You know I will, why I have to."

"Wwwwwwhy?"

"Because you're not worth keeping alive. You're excess baggage. You don't have the ruby, I don't need a hostage. You *don't* have it, do you?"

"I jus' tol' you . . ."

"Turn out your pockets."

He did so. Ben fanned him down, looking for a secret pocket. There was none. No lump, no trace of the ruby. He had no hat to search. No luggage, only an ancient, warped billfold with his through ticket and eleven paper dollars. Ben gave it back to him.

"Let's go for a walk."

"Where to? What you gonna do?"

"You'll find out when I do it."

"Whatta ya wanta kill me for? I ain' done nothin', this is my honest to God firs' time ever steppin' off the straight an' narrow. I got a weak heart . . ."

"Let's go, Frank."

"How d'you know my name? What are you, Wells Fargo?"

"U.S. Secret Service."

His jaw sagged. "Damn, you are aren'tcha? What'll happen to me?"

"For murder and robbery, what do you think?"

"I didn' murder nobody! Never in my life. I can git witnesses to prove I'm really a good soul deep down . . ."

"You and your friend are accessories to murder. As guilty as if you pulled the trigger. Let's go."

● ● ● ●

Unka timpe-wa-wince-pock-ich, the Paiute Indians called it.

"Red-rocks-standing-like-men-in-a-bowl-shaped-canyon." Sixty different shades of red were the rocks. In every conceivable shape; fantastic figures. The canyon was entered at the rim with several trails leading down to the floor. From the top of any, one could be seen domes, spires, and temples, in shades of red, pink, and cream. Grotesque. Bizarre. Weird.

It was an amphitheater hollowed and carved by the devil's hand. Or by a god's with a mischievous, devilish streak. A thirty-mile-wide workshop of an ancient sculptor, gigantic in size and ambition. A futuristic work of art; left uncompleted, its creator defeated by the splendor of the challenge.

At Bert's first glance, it appeared that immense tubes of pink and red paint had been squeezed upward from the canyon floor and turned to stone. A wildly Gothic city, the gorgeous ruins of cathedrals and castles and temples; mosques, pantheons and pagodas. Here a squatting lion. There a rampant dragon; gargoyles and basilisks, idols and heathen gods, rendered imperfect under the assault of wind and weather. Shafts, towers, spires, steeples, bulkheads, capitals, and entablatures. Suggesting the craftmanship of long-dead sculptors. Turrets and newels and facades, the works of geniuses wrought eons before.

Sunlight created a kaleidoscope of color. The stones lightened or darkened as the sun vanished behind a cloud or was partially obscured by one. Dull orange became brilliant yellow. A towering red statue of a nameless deity became almost vermilion. Then gradually brightened to vivid crimson. Golden domes flashed and sparkled, a continually shifting pattern of indescribable beauty.

Paiute legend claimed that the canyon was originally built as a city for the people of the Coyote—the birds, animals, lizards, and those that looked like men. The Coyote people displeased Coyote because they worked too long and too zealously beautifying their city. Coyote became angry; he upended their paint buckets; he turned the people to stone. There they stand to this day, stone rows and crowds of them, their faces painted with the war paint Coyote angrily hurled at them.

Bert stood on the rim looking down. His horse stood stock-still beside him. Below him somewhere was Cutler. He was certain. He had spotted his dust not once but three times since Circleville. Cutler, no one else, no one coming or going or crossing the scrub-littered wasteland. No one on the road in the distance to his right. The dust had to be raised by Cutler's mount.

But now, standing looking down into the city of stone, he saw no dust. He heard no sound. He picked up a rock and threw it as far as he could. He grimaced against the pain it started in his side. It landed far below; it clicked loudly, the echo resounding, carrying upward to him. Any hoofbeat down there would sound like a hammer striking an anvil.

He froze. The realization gripped him. Cutler was not

below. He felt it, *knew* it. His mind whirled; he'd seen he was being followed. Could even have recognized who it was. He had pulled off and hidden behind a rock.

And watched him pass! Was now behind him, framing him in his sights.

A shot cracked. The slug whistled past. Bert let go of the reins and threw himself flat. He landed on a sharp stone; it jabbed hard against his incision. He yelped in pain and pulled away the stone. The pain persisted.

"Skunk!"

He got out his gun. A second shot. Closer, on his other side. The two bracketed him. A third would split the bracket and punch his ticket if it came in low enough. He snaked backward. Feeling with his toes for the edge and the start of the trail down. He found it; he scrambled down under the rim. Just in time. Three more shots came at him, the last one through his hat.

"Jeez! . . ."

A rifle; he could tell by the sound. Sharp, light, the song of power on the fly. Power to plow through whatever it hit. And with it Cutler had his six-gun.

Bert looked up at his horse; she was standing where he'd left her. Would the mangy scum shoot her? Maybe. Any man who could gun down an unarmed woman would hardly hesitate with a dumb animal. Knowing that without his horse he'd be done for. In this country, this sun, his condition.

"No question . . ."

"EGBERRRRRRRT!"

He sounded very close; twenty feet away.

"Egbert. It's you, ain't it? I reco'nized ya, the way you sit your mount. Like a sack o' barley with a hat. Ha ha. Bowed back, all slump. I coulda' killed you passin' me, but I didn'. Wouldn' be no fun in that, would there? You listenin', Egbert?"

I hear, you mangy scum. Damned if I'll tell ya' . . .

"Egbert, I purely admire your sand, trackin' me all this way. You're somethin', but then you gotta grudge that's somethin' else, ain' that so? You're wrong, you know. I wasn't nowheres near the Cedar City road that day back when. Didn' pull no holdup. Didn' kill your missus. Never laid eyes on the lady. The bald truth is I was down to Mexico that whole month. Guanajuato. Egbert?''

"Pig. Crawlin' vermin . . ."

"You hear me? I didn't do it. Hey, was she purty? I'd never kill a purty gal. 'Nough ugly ones 'round. Ha ha. Right?''

Furious, Bert pushed upward. He fired wildly, emptying his gun. The sound of the last shot was dying away when Cutler spoke.

"What you shootin' at, Egbert? The wind? Must be, you didn' come close to this ol' boy. Cain't hit what you cain't see, right? Why don' I make it easy for you? How about I close in? Give you a look anna chance. Whatta ya say? Hol' your breath, Egbert, here I come . . .''

Bert had reloaded. He fumbled in his haste, dropping two cartridges. They rolled a ways down the grade and stopped. He cocked and rose slowly. Two quick shots sang at him. The second knocked his hat off.

"Jeez . . ."

He flattened again; he looked up at his horse. She stood head low, eyes wide with fear. The breeze sifted lightly through her mane. He click-clicked out of the side of his mouth. He got her eye.

"Here, little girl, come on down." She round-eyed him and looked away. Click click. "Come down here, dummy!''

She started forward, the reins dragging dust. She came to within four feet of him. He was up on his knees; he reached to catch the reins. Cutler let fly. The slug struck Bert's gun; it knocked it free. It slid across the ground to rest well out of reach. He cursed; he snatched the reins and pulled the horse down out of range below him.

"Stay . . ."

He crabbed back up to the rim. He eased to his right. His gun was within easy reach. He grabbed for it; Cutler held his fire. Weapon in hand, Bert started back down. He stopped and stiffened. His heart dropped.

The slug had struck the barrel at the point where it joined the recoil shield and frame. It was badly bent. Useless.

* * * *

The engine hooted up the way. Littlejohn was walking ahead of Ben. He stumbled often; he sweat furiously; his breath came in short, nervous gasps. His complexion was sallow with fear. When Ben tapped his shoulder to get his attention he all but jumped from his boots.

"Let's go back."

Relief spread over the little man's face. His eyes gave him away, welling with relief. He was not going to be killed; not here, not now. Ben smiled inwardly. Scaring him half to death was a dirty trick but necessary. It got him off balance before they even boarded the train. Got him frightened for his life; reminded him who had the gun and just might use it. He should stay in line now all the way to San Francisco.

Ben clapped his shoulder; he gripped hard.

"Be a good boy, Frank. Behave yourself, do as your told, and you'll live to a ripe old age."

He grinned feebly.

"All the way to Frisco."

His face fell. "Thennnn what?"

"Let's go, let's get on."

* * * *

Bert led the horse down the trail. He mounted at the bottom; he rode between rock formations, heading up a narrow avenue to the mouth of a cave. There were dozens all about him. He glanced back up at the rim; no sign of Cutler.

But he was coming.

He got the horse inside. The ceiling was lower than it looked from outside; barely high enough to accommodate the horse. He ducked slightly entering. Inside, he laced the reins around a stone.

"If you'd come when I'd called I wouldn' be in this fix now, stupid lookin' hayburner!"

The grulla swished her tail. As if his words were a compliment. He grinned and ruffled her mane. Then he again examined his gun. It was useless. Totally. He could try to straighten it. Lay the muzzle against a rock and stomp it. Be very careful.

It never worked. It needed proper truing at the hands of a competent gunsmith. He emptied the chamber and threw it away. He went to the mouth of the cave; he raised his hand, holding it against the top. The movement tugged his incision. He ran a hand under his shirt, feeling it. It was rough, hard as stone and sore to the touch. Running a fever. He felt his forehead; it was damp. Fear sweat or fever?

"Little o' both, prob'ly."

He had enough food and water for two or three days, if he didn't make a pig of himself. The canyon offered no grass he could see. There were only sparsely scattered small pines. The horse could get by without food for at least another twenty-four hours. But for what Cutler had in mind, nothimg like that length of time would be needed.

It'd be all over before dark.

Bert cocked an ear. The breeze whined as it slipped through the tall rock towers. The only sound in the silent city. He could not look for Cutler to come down the trail he himself had taken. Was he aware that his last shot had ruined his Classic? Most likely. He'd sounded very close; he should have been able to see.

Bert went back past the horse; he struck a match. There might be a rear way out, he thought. He started back; the ceiling dipped even lower and for about ten strides the cave narrowed. Then it widened, the ceiling rose, and there was a turning to the left. He lit his third and last match and eased around it. The stink of rotten meat and feces struck his nostrils. Tiny, twin yellow lights glowed in the darkness just ahead. There came a low, gutteral sound.

He dropped the match; he whirled about and was halfway back around the corner, his fingers scraping the rugged wall, when the cougar charged roaring. She flashed by him, so close her shoulder brushed him. He ran. He jerked out his knife and grabbed the reins as he passed the horse. The cat came bounding after. He threw a look behind him. She had reached the innermost fringe of daylight flooding into the cave. He saw clearly her small, sand-colored head, the black ears, muzzle, and lower lip. Her huge, fearsome teeth bared. Again she leaped. Slamming into the defenseless horse's rump. It whinnied in pain, kicked, and tumbled the cat. She scrambled to her feet.

He whirled; he stabbed wildly; he caught her high up on the neck, the blade thrusting deep, snapping bone. Down she fell; she twisted about enraged, roaring viciously. Back through the interior the sound echoed.

Bert two-handed the knife, blade upward. He pushed with all his strength; he stabbed her just under the throat, then into it. Again! Again! She rocked her head side to side trying to dislodge the knife. His third upward stroke he held in place; lifted her bodily vertical; tipped her head over heels and free of the knife. She landed on her back. Over she rolled on one side, the fur at and beneath her throat dark and shining with blood. A crimson bib spreading, enlarging as it seeped from the severed arteries. In her eyes was a glassy stare. She kicked, twitched, and lay still.

He dropped the bloodied knife and knelt. He ran his hand over her chest. She was dead. He examined the horse's rump. Five slender crimson slashes chevroned each side of it. The blood glistened as it surfaced, but the gougings did not appear deep. He got out his bandanna, wet it, and wiped her down. The cloth absorbed little blood. He gave her water from his hat.

He restored his canteen to the pommel of his saddle and abruptly realized how severe the pain of his incision had become. He lifted his shirt to examine it. In his exertions he had ripped it two-thirds open. He could see no fresh blood. He lay the tips of his fingers against the afflicted area. It was on fire.

"Jeez . . ."

The city outside swam briefly before his eyes; his knees felt weak. He swayed and stretched out a hand to brace himself against the horse. Slowly, gradually, the red and pink towers outside grew sharp and clear again.

"EGBERRRRRRRT!"

He moved to the cave mouth; he chanced a look out and upward at the rim. What he could see of it without stepping outside. He saw nothing. At his feet lay a small stone. He stiffened, holding his upper body straight, knelt, and picked up the stone. He held his incision with one hand and threw the stone as far as he could. It clattered to rest. Two shots rang; dust kicked up near where it landed.

"Egberrrrt!"

Back from the entrance Bert shrank. He listened. Steps. To his left. They continued, then stopped. And resumed. Slower. It was hard to pinpoint their exact location. He eased forward; one quick look. They *were* off to his left. Or were they?

He paused to ponder. Up jumped Cutler like a jack-in-the-box released. Squarely before him, not twenty yards distant. Rifle cocked. Aimed at his face.

"Egbert. Ha ha, whatta ya know. Its been awhile..."

On he came. He stopped less than twenty-five feet away. "Where's your gun?"

"As if you din' know." Bert raised his hands.

"You lost it? Ha. It wouldn' be stuck in your belt roun' behind you, would it? You wouldn' try a motheaten ol' trick like that on me, would you?"

"Why don'tcha just shut up an' get it over with..."

"So it is gone. Busted up, eh? Shame. That puts you plumb outta' picture cards. This just ain't your lucky day. Still, I don' much like shootin' a unarmed man."

"Then don't."

"You ain't givin' me much choice..."

"How about I make it easy an' turn my back?"

"That ain't very nice to say. How you been, Egbert? How's the worl' been treatin' you since..., where was it las'? Las Palomas, New Mexico, right?"

He smirked in triumph. To Bert he looked as if he were holding back a cheer. His single eye narrowed slowly, evilly. His empty right socket looked exactly the same color as the Dragon's Eye. Close up, Bert could see that he hadn't changed any since last they'd seen one another. Greasy hair a little longer, perhaps. But no heavier, no lighter. His clothes even seemed to be the same. It had been nearly eighteen months.

"'Fraid I'm gonna have to do it, Egbert. We both know it

hadda fall one way or t'other. 'Pears like it's my way. All mine. Man gets himself a chance like this, the full, complete drop on his enemy, he's a fool not to take 'vantage of it.''

He had let the rifle drop as he came closer. Down came the muzzle, aiming at Bert's feet. He raised it. The empty black eye under the front sight gaped at him.

"Get it over with, why don'tcha?"

"You invitin' me to? Don' be in sucha rush. Don' worry, I'll kill you alright. An' gladly. Hap'ly. There's jus' one li'l bit o' what you might call unfinished business twixt you an' me. I tol' you up top, tol' you before las' year. Tol' you lots o' times. I never did shoot your missus.''

"You're a liar!"

"I DIDN'!"

"Six witnesses described you to a tee."

"What six witnesses . . . ?"

"Rest o' the passengers."

"My my, is thatta fact? Never thought 'bout them. Hey, if they're that sure, maybe it *was* me who killed her.'' He laughed lightly.

"PIG!"

Cutler sobered. "Was a accident. Had to be. I don' go 'roun' gunnin' down shemales in col' blood. I don'.''

"Did she make it enjoyable for you? Did she have her hands up?"

"She likely sassed me. I was mad. On my high ropes. Anybody mouths me I gives 'em what for. So do you. So does everybody.''

"Murderin' scum.''

"Goodbye, Egbert.''

His face hardened; his body stiffened; his trigger finger started back.

Three quick shots. Down from above they winged. Cutler froze; his one working eye widened, staring. Two more shots. He swung about and ran, dodging between pillars and spires. Slugs hurried him on his way. Dumfounded by the interruption, shocked, unable to move, Bert followed him with his eyes. In seconds he was lost from sight far to the right. Among steeples and towers.

Seconds later Bert heard the sharp clacking of hooves. Retreating. His sight obscured by the multitude of stones he could see neither man or horse.

Someone was coming: Mr. Johnny-on-the-spot. Down the trail he had come down earlier. He appeared. He was tall, swarthy-looking. His six-gun smoked in his hand. Bert recognized him. The man grinned, waved, and shoved his gun into his holster. His sling was gone, but his wrist was still bandaged. The injury incurred in the train wreck.

Bert returned his smile. Then his eyes drifted from him, drawn away by the dying sound of his departing enemy. Cutler. He'd left him alive, his hatred and hunger for vengeance intact. To simmer in his soul till next they met. As they would.

To try again to settle the score.

Thirteen

Henry Olcott. Bert shook his head in wonderment.

"You . . ."

"In the flesh."

"You followed us clear down . . ."

"Looks that way, doesn't it?"

"How come?"

Olcott laughed. "To save your life, it seems."

"It's crazy."

"I'm here. Want to pinch me, see if I'm real?"

"Where's your sidekick?"

"On his way to Frisco. He's supposed to be, that's the plan." He paused, cocked his head, and eyed him. "You look peaked. Sick. I saved your life, Mr. Slaughter."

"Yeah . . ."

"You'll keep that in mind later on, won't you?"

"What are you talkin' about?"

Bert was tempted to pinch himself. He just could be dreaming. Had been, from as far back as Circleville.

Again Olcott grinned. "It can wait." He looked in the direction Cutler had taken. "Sorry he got away. Old friend of yours?"

"Sorta'. Whatta you say, how's 'bout handin' it over. Make it easy on yourself."

"The ruby?"

"What else?"

"Sorry, I don't have it."

"You got it. Give it here."

"You think I'm lying?" Olcott shook his head. He suddenly looked hurt to the quick. "That's not very nice. I just saved your life. Another two seconds and he would have blown you away."

Again the silent city floated before Bert's eyes. He sucked air. So deeply his incision twinged. The scene steadied.

"You'd better sit down," said Olcott.

Bert sat. "It's the heat..."

Olcott approached. "Search me, Mr. Slaughter. You find the ruby, I'll eat it."

"Never mind."

"I insist."

He patted himself down. He turned his pockets out, took off his boots, and poured out sand. He took off his hat and ran his finger inside the lining. And studied Bert.

"You really are sick. In pain?"

"'S my operation."

"What operation?"

Bert pulled up his shirt. Olcott examined the incision.

"It's badly infected. It's got to be attended to. You'll be in big trouble if it's not taken care of. Got any salt?"

"A little."

"Make a saltwater solution. Wash it. Carefully. It may not get rid of the infection, but it should keep it from spreading." He paused; his handsome face darkened. "We've got to keep you alive. We've a long trip ahead of us."

Bert stared mystified.

"I'd better explain."

"This oughta be good..."

"Please hear me out. Why do you think I split with Frank? Why would I follow you clear down here? Because you, Mr. Slaughter, are my ace in the hole."

"You got it backwards, you're mine..."

Olcott shook his head. "You don't understand. I've changed my mind. Jethro changed it for me. When he gunned down that mail-car clerk. Robbery's one thing. Murder, no thanks. The way you came after Frank and me, by the time we got to

Gypsum I knew it was as good as over for us. The others were already behind bars; it'd just be a matter of time before you got us. You and your partner. If not you, somebody else. Everybody with a badge was jumping into the thing.

"I want to make a deal with you, Mr. Slaughter. My neck in exchange for the ruby. I can lead you straight to it. Hand it over to you. You let me walk."

Bert shook his head. "Not a chance. I wouldn' if I could, an' I can't. I'm just a workin' stiff, I don' call the shots. Not the big ones, like who goes down an' who doesn'..."

"You could testify for me. You'd testify for the man who saved your life, wouldn't you?"

"Brother, I'm ailin', but I'm not stupid. Do I look to you like I'm fresh off the farm or what? I've heard Class-A bull in my time..."

"No bull. We're talking about my life." He pulled his gun. Bert tensed. Olcott handed it to him butt first. "Take it. Keep it all the way to Frisco. You'll be in charge. When we get there I'll take you straight to the ruby. It's yours, Mr. Slaughter. With my blessing."

"You're fixin' to double-cross Littlejohn..."

"He won't get hurt. He'll be disappointed, but that's the way it goes. My neck is worth more than money in his pocket. He won't miss what he's never had. Take my gun, Mr. Slaughter."

Bert holstered it. He stared. Olcott's face was masked with sincerity. His tone, his manner appeared completely genuine. Still, Bert thought, he was *not* fresh off the farm. Olcott could sell till he was blue in the face, he wasn't about to buy. Not yet. Maybe never.

"We've got to ride clear to Modena, almost the Nevada border. Close to a hundred and twenty miles. Think you'll be up to it? Modena's the nearest train, the San Pedro, Los Angeles, and Salt Lake. It'll take us north to Lake Point across from Salt Lake City. We can switch over there to the Western Pacific. We'll be in San Francisco by Monday.

"But before we do anything else, let's get you to the nearest doctor. Orton's about five miles west of here. Here, let me help you..."

• • • •

Ben and Frank Littlejohn had changed trains a second time in Wetts, Nevada. They would take the Southern Pacific across Nevada to California and the Sierra. Through the San Joaquin Valley to San Francisco. Ben sat beside the little man listening patiently to his whining about his health. His claim to an unblemished record as an upstanding citizen before joining the gang. His first straying from the path of righteousness. Ben almost felt sorry for him.

"You got to unnerstan', Mr. Slaughter, makin' a livin' is hard for a nothin' little man like me. Bein' smaller than the other fella cuts a man outta' a whole passel o' jobs. Can't punch cattle, ain't much good 'round a farm or ranch; bosses is allus got their eye out for big, strappin' young fellas. Tried to make it with the railroad, but that's a good job evvybody's after an' others allus seem to get. I could stan' in line for the next ten years waitin' for a break there. Not big nor strong 'nough to work minin'. I can drive a wagon or stagecoach right 'nough, but so can evvybody else, women even. Just no drivin' jobs 'round. I thought 'bout clerkin' in a store or bein' a bank teller. I scrubbed up clean, shaved, bought myself a two-buck boiled shirt an' necktie. Had a good flannel suit, store bought, but nobody'll hire me. My bigges' trouble is I can't read nor write."

"Didn't you go to school?"

"Never seen the inside o' no schoolhouse ever. Maw an' Paw, my four brothers, sister Vira an' me lived on sixty-two acres o' sugar-beet patch up to Montana Territory. Soil was so poor you couldn' hardly grow weeds. We'da like to starve to death if it warn't for the neighbors. Worked like mules, all of us, barely made 'nough to live. Didn' have time for school, nor church, nothin' but bust our backs in the fields. An' my paw an' maw was both kilt when the barn c'lapsed on 'em. Crushed 'em to death. I wasn' but nine year old. Oldest was Clydell, sixteen. He kep' us together, kep' us workin' the beets. Then Walter, the secon' oldes', come down with the grippe. So bad he died. Life can be merciless hard for them with no luck, no chances, no one to help give 'em a leg up. Know what I mean?''

''So you turned to crime.''

''Didn' turn nothin'. Orland Bisby an' Jethro come to me. Ast me iff'n I wanted in. I was flat broke, no job, no horse, nothin' but the clothes on my back. And them wore down 'most to rags. It was highline ride or starve to death.''

The train had slowed since leaving Verdi. Crossing over into California and starting up into the Sierra. The day was clear and reasonably cool for midsummer; the scenery was magnificent. On chattered Frank Littlejohn. Ben had wearied of his tireless prattle but did feel sorry for him. His story was that of ten thousand others. He hadn't been forced into a life of crime. He'd backed into it. Still, the choice was his; nobody had coerced him. Though in a sense life itself had.

He didn't have the ruby. Olcott must. Littlejohn insisted he did. If he was lying, if it was sitting in some post office waiting for them to pick it up, he was putting on a first-rate show of innocence and honesty. Whatever the case, he resolved to stick to him like Diamond Liquid Glue. Littlejohn would lead him straight to Olcott and the stone. Littlejohn wouldn't dare try to deceive him; he was too frightened to.

The whistle hooted. Ben wondered why it was sounded. At the rate they were moving, a blind and crippled pregnant cow could move out of the way before the cowcatcher nudged her.

•   •   •   •

The doctor washed the incision with a weak solution of carbolic acid. Though not as weak as Bert would have liked. The sting of it temporarily erased the soreness. And set him sweating, despite clamping his teeth so tightly on a tongue depressor he broke it. New stitches were inserted to close the gaping lower half of the cut. The doctor applied a salve but did not put on a fresh dressing.

''Best to let the air get at it. Keep your shirt open if you can. Careful you don't let any dust or dirt get in.'' He handed him the tube. ''Rub a little on it every night and every morning when you get up.''

"What is it?"

"Salve."

"I can see that!"

"Would you recognize it if I told you?"

"Try me."

"Multistrength Chemical Opodeldoc Salve."

Bert grunted.

"It acts as a shield against infection. Do yourself a favor, keep your dirty hands off it."

"They're not dirty!"

"They're not exactly immaculate. Let me ask you something, who took out your appendix? It's possible I know him..."

"A guy named Fizz something..."

"Frizz...," corrected Olcott. He caught himself and stopped. The doctor glanced at him. Bert ignored him.

"It's a fairly large incision. I would have cut half the size. What was he, the local vet?"

"He was a doctor, for Godsakes!"

"Alright, alright, don't get upset. That'll be two dollars."

Olcott paid him before Bert could reach into his pocket.

They stood outside. The sun was so huge, so fiery, it seemed as if the earth had drawn closer to it. And would soon be consumed by its merciless rays. The sweltering air seemed to vibrate.

Bert wondered why Olcott had paid the doctor, but not enough to discuss it. Never look a gift horse in the mouth, he thought.

"He looked more like a mortician than a doctor. Ever see anybody so skinny in your life? With that waxy skin he had on he looked like a cadaver." He shuddered.

"He seemed to know what he was doing."

"Filthy office. Hasn' been swept out in seven years, I betcha. All them open bottles, the stinks, the bloody gauze in the wastebasket. It's 'nough to make a man puke."

A fly passed. Two pretty girls who looked like sisters shared the seat. Bert tipped his hat. They smiled, looked at each other, and tittered. He got out the salve. There was no label. He unscrewed the top and smelled it.

"Smells like horse liniment."

"Do you feel up to riding?"

"You kiddin'? I gotta iron constitution. I could ride clear to 'laska, if I had to. Lead on . . ."

Bert followed him to where they'd hitched their horses. He eyed the back of Olcott's neck. His hand drifted to the gun. He would stick to him like Diamond Liquid Glue from here to Frisco. Let him lead him to little big ears and the Dragon's Eye. Until he got it in the palm of his hand, he wouldn't let Olcott out of his sight!

"Things are lookin' up."

"You say something?" Olcott turned around. His eyes questioned.

"Nothin'."

Cutler jumped into his thoughts. He'd had him, he'd lost him. Rather Cutler had had him. Cold. Olcott *had* saved his hide, no question. He'd be lying dead in the main street of the silent city waiting for the circling birds if he hadn't shown up.

Where had Cutler gotten to, he wondered. Into Arizona by now. Down into Mexico by day after tomorrow. He had his share of the holdup loot; from how many holdups before that one?

Would their paths ever cross again? They would; he'd see to it. And next time the boot would be on the other foot. He'd get the drop. Cutler'd had his chance and blown it. Talked too much, too long. He'd never get another chance like it.

"Amen to that."

Again Olcott turned and looked.

"Nothin', nothin'."

Fourteen

In San Francisco, where the city and hills meet the sea, there is a street. The Embarcadero. It starts in the freight yards, where the warehouses and squat little factories stand near the Southern Pacific depot. From there it runs north for nearly two blocks. It then curves northwest, then west, bending again with the outward curve of the waterfront. It continues westward until it stops abruptly at the fishing boats, drying crab nets, and hole-in-the-wall restaurants of Fisherman's Wharf. Here the sea laps the gray timbers of the piers. Here the city wears the weary drab of all waterfronts in all the ports of the world. Here was where Frank Littlejohn led Ben Slaughter. Dinning his ears with continuing fervent declarations of cooperation. No reformed drunk, no finder and embracer of Christ was ever more sincere.

"You can trus' me, Mr. Slaughter. You can. So help me. I jus' don' wanna hang. I'll go to jail for twenny years, only don' let 'em hang me. Please . . ."

Ben made no promises. The only assurance he gave was silently. And to himself. He'd gotten the little man off-balance; he would keep him there until the ruby was recovered. How long they would have to wait for Olcott, Littlejohn had no idea. Ben had assumed he would be there waiting for his partner when they arrived. So thought Littlejohn. He seemed surprised when they arrived at the Java Hotel and Olcott wasn't there to greet them.

The Java Hotel was a disreputable-looking, four-story shack, frequented by a host of the most unsavory-looking types Ben had ever seen collected in one place. Mostly sailors and their ladies of the evening and elderly fishermen cast up onto the beach by their age and infirmities. Living out their lives in poverty and neglect among their kind. Everyone Ben saw looked utterly defeated. No smiles, no laughter, no hint whatsoever that a single one was satisfied, much less happy to be alive.

One glimpse of the building outside and he pictured the cellar overrun with rats, armies of cockroaches maneuvering on all four floors, filth, squalor, and stink everywhere. His imagination exaggerated only slightly.

They took a room on the third floor. After turning down two others on the floor below. Ben sat on the bed testing it as Littlejohn closed and locked the door.

"What is that stink?" Ben asked.

"Dead fish. You'll get used to it."

"I take it you've been here before . . ."

"Couple years back. I drifted out here lookin' for work. I'm all the time lookin'. I had a idee I'd try fishin', but it was no soap. Fishin', crabbin', shrimpin' an' suchlike is family businesses. You got to be Eyetalian or a Chinee . . ."

Ben smiled. "Couldn't you get yourself shanghaied? Get steady work aboard a freighter?"

"I thought about it. I did. The money wouldn' be much. The work'd be killin', but I'd get my meals. An' a warm hammock. And make frien's. Only I couldn' take the sea. The rollin' o' the waves makes me sicker'n a dog."

Ben looked about. The walls and floor were bare pine. A rickety little table sat beside the iron bed. There was no lamp, only a candle stub. Planted on the table. Two grimy windows looked out over the tar-papered roof of the warehouse next door. Beyond it gulls wheeled over the unseen water.

"What a lovely home away from home."

"I know. I'm sorry, but this is where we're s'posed to make contac' with the Australian fella."

"How much is he going to give you for the ruby?"

"Dunno. Henry knows; Henry's got a head for bus'ness. He can cipher an' evvythin'. He's smart as a whip."

"I'm sure. Frank, I'm hungry."

"Me, too."

Ben got three dollars out of his billfold. "Get us something hot if you can. Meat, fish, whatever. Get some fruit, too. And see if you can find a bottle of cold milk."

The sun came up on the little man's face. He beamed.

"You *do* trus' me now, don'tcha?"

"What do you think? You'd better not run out on me. Oh, you might get away, but if you don't . . ."

His face, as high up on his head as he could raise it, fell. "Whyn'cha come with me after the food?"

"What do you need me for?"

"It's gettin' dark out. This is a rough neighborhood. You got the guns . . ."

Ben sighed. When they had walked through the station after getting off the train, his heart had been in his mouth. For fear somebody from the office would spot him. Just his luck Lloyd Tevis himself would come marching up. He had walked swiftly to the nearest hansom; he'd held his hat partially over his face. Which may have drawn attention, but at least hid his identity.

They left the hotel. Night came slinking across the bay into the city. The docked fishing boats nudged the street with their stubby prows, their lights blooming high above. The soft lapping of water against the pilings resembled music. The warm air carried the smell of saltwater. A bell rang mournfully in the distance; it carried low over the water from out where the tides ran swiftly past Yerba Buena Island and the Island of Angels. Lights twinkled on the inland hills and a dim amber glow crowned the city.

The stink of dead fish set Ben's stomach in rebellion against seafood. He set his heart on a steak, potatoes, vegetables—a full and decent meal. Most welcome after all the quick cold bites and tepid, bitter coffee consumed en route.

They turned into Howard Street. They came upon a small

restaurant, but famished as he was, it was too busy, too crowded and noisy for his liking. On they strolled.

"If I recollec' rightly, they's a chophouse jus' roun' the next corner."

They started around the corner. Ben hurried his step. A man approached. Out of simple curiosity, Ben lifted his eyes to look at his face in the yellow glow of the gas lamp.

He was tall, over six feet, unusually broad shouldered. He was handsome; he wore a neatly clipped mustache. He recognized Ben the instant he recognized him. His face exploded in a furious expression.

"Benjamin!"

"Good evening, Chief Hu. . . . Hume."

Fifteen

Ben fought back his fluster. He squared his shoulders; tried to look the picture of confidence; failed utterly. Stupid words blurted forth.

"Fancy meeting you here."

"Fancy indeed." Hume stared through him. "Aren't you going to introduce me?"

Ben suddenly remembered Littlejohn was standing at his elbow. "This is Frank. Frank, go get something to eat. I'll catch you later."

"I . . ., sure."

Off he went.

"Pleasant evening, isn't it?" said Hume.

He filled his massive chest; and let it out slowly. He continued to rivet Ben with his eyes.

"I can explain everything, Chief."

"Not here on a street corner. Let's find us a nice, quiet booth in a halfway-decent restaurant."

● ● ● ●

They sat in a corner booth. The restaurant was small, stuffy, crowded. Only slightly less noisy than the one Ben and Littlejohn had passed up on Howard Street. Between them sat two steins of beer. Hume's eyes continued to bore relentlessly. He drank, tsk-tsked, sucked a tooth, and resumed boring.

"Let's start out with the cards face up. You and your father have been fired."

"For failure to recover the ruby?"

"Ther's more to it than that and you know it!" Hume pounded the table, setting both steins dancing.

"For not contacting you? With what? To tell you we were still on the job? Didn't you assume we were? There wasn't anything else to tell."

"That's not the point."

"The point is Tevis is embarrassed. He's up in arms. He's got to take it out on somebody. Good. Fine. We're fired, no longer associated with the company. We're on our own. Two public-spirited citizens dedicated to recovering King Leopold's ruby. And wiping out the smudge on the nation's escutcheon. Restoring its honor. *And* collecting the ten thousand reward."

"Balderdash! As if either of you cared about the money . . ."

Ben drank. He returned his stare with equal intensity. "Don't fool yourself, Chief. We'll take it. Happily. What you fail to understand is that we <u>know</u> where the ruby is. And we'll get it back. When we do, neither you or Tevis, no one with Wells Fargo will see it. Will even know. We'll march the bloody thing straight to Washington. Turn it over to the secretary of state. Maybe even the president himself, and with a couple hundred newspaper reporters looking on. No sense taking any chances Unconditional Surrender might renege on the reward."

"You wouldn't do that."

"What choice are you giving us?"

"Where's Egbert?"

"What do you care? What does Wells Fargo care if he's alive or dead? And he could very easily be dead. What with all he's been put through *in the line of duty.*"

The last word emerged accompanied by a scowl that implied a viciously bitter taste.

"Calm down. You blame me for that? Or Mr. Tevis? You're assignment was to guard the collection . . ."

Ben lay a coin on the table and got to his feet.

"Sit down, Benjamin, I'm not finished."

"I am. Good night, Chief. Goodbye. It's been a pleasure working for you. Seriously. I'm sorry it has to end like this."

"SIT DOWN! Please . . . And please keep your voice down. Our problems are nobody's business. Listen to me, firing you two wasn't my idea. I think it stinks to high heaven."

"You listen. We both knew he'd get around to it as far back as Gypsum. It figures with him." He shrugged. "He's in charge, he does as he pleases."

"I repeat, I think it stinks. His mind's made up to press charges against you."

"For not wiring you?"

"He came stomping into my office this morning and announced that he was absolutely convinced that you two are in cahoots with the thieves. You've turned your coats. I hit the ceiling. Not that I thought it would change his thinking. To set him straight on how I felt. As if he cared." Again he sipped; he wiped the foam from his mouth. His voice seemed to be tiring. He looked tired. "I intend to resign."

Ben blanched. "Hold everything."

"I can't stand by and see him do this to you. It's not you, per se. It's not even this case, what you've done, what you haven't. It's the principle. If, whenever the bottom drops out of a case, he takes it as an excuse to destroy the people involved, if he fires his intelligence and puts his temper in charge, *everybody becomes a potential victim.* I can only speak for myself, but I can't do my job with the sword of Damocles hanging over me. Who can? Why should anyone have to?"

"I understand what you're saying. I just don't think Bert'll like the idea of your resigning on account of us. I don't. We may have had our differences in the past, but . . . James, we don't want you quitting. I don't want it on my conscience."

"It's got nothing to do with either of you."

"It's got everything."

"Benjamin, I admire your father. I respect him. Deep down you know I do. Only I can never talk to him. Not like you. He's . . . too emotional."

"He's a hotheaded, pigheaded, crackbrained idiot. At times."

Hume smiled. First of the evening. "Put Egbert and Tevis

in the same room and they'd murder each other. And yet, for all Tevis's vanity, his iciness, his woeful lack of humanity, his failure to see beyond his nose, as in this thing, his . . . think of every negative, it'll suit, he's good for the company. He's got more drive than any five men I've ever known. Considerably more than Henry Wells or Bill Fargo, both of whom I dearly love.

"Over the past eleven years, Tevis has built this company into the largest and most successful company of its type in the world. He's made mistakes, making a gigantic one with you and your dad, he's alienated people, crossed and double-crossed, he's gambled, he's lost, he's won, he's failed, he's triumphed. But he's never given up. Never backed away from a fight. Never quit. The man's a giant. I can't stand the sight of him!"

"What's your point?"

"I ask you to look at his side of it. He's consumed with embarrassment over this business. He's courting a heart attack. His hands are tied; all he can do is stand helplessly by and watch the government step in and try to pull Wells Fargo's chestnuts out of the fire."

"They can't. Only Bert and I can. Grant can send fifty thousand secret service men running all over North America. The only thing they'll turn up is their expense accounts."

"I couldn't agree more. But let me go on. Oh, would you like another beer?"

"I'd rather something to eat. Before I pass out."

"Why didn't you say so? Waiter!"

They ordered steaks with all the trimmings.

"As I was saying," said Hume. "You and Egbert are fired as of the day before yesterday. Officially. Tomorrow morning I resign."

"I wish you wouldn't."

He waved this beyond consideration. "Let me tell you what I think you two ought to do."

"Drop the case."

"Exactly. What's the point in going on?"

Ben grinned. "I can think of ten thousand reasons to."

"That's blood money, you don't want it."

"It's currency of the realm. Genuine. Eminently spendable. We could live like princes. And who knows, when we've returned the ruby to His Majesty, he might decide to hire us as his personal security guards. We could end up moving to Belgium."

"Balderdash! I'm saying drop it. Oh, it's possible you'll recover the ruby. I'd bet on it. But that won't cut any ice with Tevis."

"To hell with Tevis."

"On the other hand, if you don't get it back, even if you do, you could both wind up in an alley in Chinatown with your throats cut."

"How many cases don't threaten a violent windup? You're not making much of an argument to induce us to give up. Why should we? We're already fired, we have nothing to lose with the company, everything to gain with the ruby."

Dinner arrived. They ate in silence, broken now and again by comment on the food. Not another word about the ruby, the company, Lloyd Tevis, firing, resigning, or the reward. Hume had gotten nowhere with friendly persuasion, and bulldozing was beneath him. Ben was unreceptive; he could see it, he kept his piece.

All Ben could think of at the moment was Bert. Somewhere back in Utah or by now perhaps Nevada, hurting, probably suffering, chasing or being chased by Olcott *and* Cutler. Alone. In danger . . .

To the devil with Lloyd Tevis and Wells Fargo. To the devil with Unconditional Surrender Grant and his clumsy efforts to interfere. To the devil with everybody and everything.

Except the Dragon's Eye and the ten thousand.

Sixteen

Ben left James Hume in a cordial if defeated mood. He held no brief against the man. Nor did Bert. Nevertheless, the situation and Hume's role in it saddened him. Still, he couldn't bring himself to be angry with Tevis. Couldn't be bothered. The man was what he was and had to live with himself as that. Cross enough for anyone to bear.

Fog thickly blanketed the bay. It came rolling easily, snugly into place, stretching, making its silent way into the city. Down the streets and alleys it sneaked. It dulled the feebly glowing gas lamps; it dampened the pavements and cobblestones. It brought with it a clammy chill, like a draft from the tomb. It stole into one's pores and mind. And stirred the well of loneliness.

Ben turned from Howard Street into Second. He headed toward the docks and the Java Hotel. A Rockaway carriage jiggled by, its spider-web wheels clacking lightly. The horse's hooves resounded sharply against the stones; fuzzy spheres of light imprisoned in their lamps illuminated nothing but themselves. The driver looked like Charon, the ferryman. He had exchanged his ragged garments and cap for the formal garb of stovepipe hat and cloak. And was out diligently searching the night for stray souls.

Two sailors loitered in front of the hotel. One touched his cap in greeting and stepped aside to let Ben enter. The lobby was deserted; no one was at the desk. Newspapers were strewn about and the odor of stale liquor struck him as he crossed to the stairs.

He unlocked the door, took a step, and stopped. The room was a shambles. The nightstand and chair were shattered; the dresser drawers were pulled out and overturned. The bedstead looked as if it had been struck repeatedly with a sledgehammer. The mattress was half onto the floor; it was drenched with blood.

Frank Littlejohn lay on the floor under the window. His throat cut. His pale-gray eyes stared sightlessly at the ceiling. His clothing was partially ripped from his body. One boot was off. Blood streaked the grime-encrusted window above him. Ben swallowed hard; he took a deep breath and moved into the room. He closed the door, actuating a loud clattering. He turned and saw that a hatchet had been stuck in the door and had fallen when he closed it. He bent to pick it up; he changed his mind and went to Littlejohn.

Pity surged through him. He looked about. He envisioned a giant fist snatching the room out of the building, shaking it violently, and thrusting it back into place. A fist had obviously killed Littlejohn; the one that held the knife that had slashed his throat. Whoever had done it and ransacked the place had evidently not found what they were looking for.

He left, closing and locking the door. The clerk, somebody, would find the body and summon the police. Perhaps not. Perhaps such goings-on were common practice in such a place.

Outside he gulped air and held it. The two sailors had gone. He heard a soft clicking sound to his left. Out of the swirling fog came a woman. Young. Her skirts swished lightly as she approached. Atop her head was an enormous hat, coils of silk matching her crimson and gray dress. A huge, dyed ostrich feather thrust into the crown bobbed absurdly with her every step. So large was her hat it overpowered her little face. She was pretty but wore too much makeup, eye shadow and rouge igniting her cheeks like little lanterns. On she came, bringing with her the scent of lilac. She smiled.

"Bon soir, monsieur . . ."

"Good evening." He tipped his hat.

"I am lost, I theenk. I am looking for zee Palais Hotel?"

"You're heading in the wrong direction." He pointed left. "It's back the way you came. Past Howard to Mission, turn in Mission and take your first right. You can't miss it. It's right on the corner of Mark . . ."

The last syllable did not come out. Powerful hands seized and pinned his arms behind him. A damp cloth pressed against his nose and mouth. The sickly-sweet odor of chloroform shot up his nostrils. Her smile liquified before his eyes. It spread, undulating, vanishing as the fog rolled in.

● ● ● ●

The train had stopped at the modest little depot in Belmont. It sat at the foot of gently rolling, almost treeless hills. A few minutes later they pulled into Union Station. It was not yet completed but already pressed into service. The time was fourteen minutes past eight in the evening.

Bert could not have asked for a friendlier, more interesting traveling companion than Henry Olcott. For hours on end Olcott regaled him with fascinating stories of his travels in South America. And his adventures placer mining gold in Colorado. From his manner of speaking, his skill with words, Bert might have taken him for a college professor or lawyer rather than the bugheway he was. It struck him as strange that a man of his so-obvious intelligence and education would team with someone like Littlejohn. But the lure of a fast buck made for many an unusual partnership.

He had come to like Olcott. And not just for saving his life. Not even because he'd gotten him to Doctor Cadaver in Orton to tend to his incision. He just basically liked him: his frankness, openness. He was a man's man, easy to talk to, enjoyable to be with.

He liked him but was not at all tempted to trust him. And wasn't about to be lulled by his charm into letting down his guard. On the ride west, Olcott didn't harp on his change of heart regarding the Dragon's Eye. He wasn't looking for compliments or gratitude or encouragement. All he wanted was for Bert to testify for him. Even before they boarded the train in Modena, Bert leveled with him. He'd have to wait and see how the cards came out of the shoe before he made any promises.

They had sold their horses and gear in Modena. Olcott insisted Bert continue to hang onto his gun. Proof of his good faith. Without his asking, Bert would have done so.

They stood together in Union Station; passengers and porters came and went in a flurry of activity. Baggage carts trundled by; hawkers dispensed everything from candy to chewing tobacco. No Battle Ax available, Bert settled for second best: a plug of Red Bull.

"Where to now?" he asked Olcott. And started on a chaw, roughly a third of the plug.

Olcott grinned and winked. "Still don't trust me, do you?"

"Should I?"

He shrugged. "I can't make you. Just keep watching, you'll see I'm on the level."

"What makes you think you can talk your little big-eared pal into givin' up the Dragon's Eye?"

"I can handle Frank."

"You trust him?"

"Implicitly. He may be crude and uneducated but he's honorable."

"He trust you?"

"I think so."

"Let's go find him. Get the friggin' thing an' this over with. Where'd you say he's at?"

"A little hotel on Second Street. Down by the docks."

"Bet you a buck my son Ben's with him. Been stickin' to him ever since Provo."

A newsboy came by waving the *Examiner*. Bert spotted a headline on the front page.

"Gimme one here, sonny."

He read: "Crown Jewels Still Missing. Wells Fargo Vows to Continue Search Despite Company's Dismissal From Case by Federal Government."

The item itself was mainly a rehash of rumors. The cow was dry, but the milkmaid refused to quit miking. He shoved the paper under his arm.

"How you figger to talk Littlejohn into this? He looks a stubborn cuss to me. He could turn you down col'."

"Possibly. I'll try every possible tack. I've made up my mind, Mr. Slaughter. Frank or nobody's going to change it. Actually, I'll be doing him as big a favor as myself."

"He might not see it that way; he don' strike me as too bright."

"When we get to the hotel, I'll go up alone, if that's okay with you."

"Ben'll be with him."

"If he is, I'll ask him to step outside. He shouldn't object. Frank and I'll talk. I'll reason with him. I'll get him to hand it over. If he doesn't . . ."

"You'll crack him one an' take it."

"Oh no, violence is not my style. If he refuses me, I'll send your son down to get you. The three of us should be able to persuade him."

"Maybe you won't have to. Ben could already have got it from him."

"Let's go."

They crossed to the main entrance. The dying sun's rays filtered through the huge Palladian window above the doors. The sidewalks were mobbed. A row of cabs was parked at the curb across the street. Even as they spied them, fares began taking them. Off they rolled, one by one. The line moved up as empty cabs drew up at the end of it.

To their right, parked at the curb just beyond the corner of the side street joining the main thoroughfare, stood two more empty cabs.

Bert pointed. "Let's get us one o' them. How far's this dive?"

"Six or seven blocks."

Olcott started off ahead of him. He was three paces in front; they began skirting the crowd on the inside. Workmen were hammering high up on scaffolding set flush with the front of the station. Olcott stepped nimbly between the upright supports; he stopped and looked back at Bert. A rumbling sounded above. A soft whooshing sound followed. Bert looked up. A plank came plummeting down. Before he could move, before he could cry out warning, it came hurtling down lengthwise; it grazed the side of Olcott's head, slammed against his shoulder, and clattered to rest.

Onlookers gasped. A woman screamed. A man yelled warning too late from above. Olcott lay with his limbs flung outward like a doll flung into a corner. He looked dead. Bert knelt and examined him; he felt his heart. It was still pumping, he was still breathing.

"Somebody get a ambulance. QUICK!"

Two policemen burst through the crowd. They brandished their nightsticks and herded the rubberneckers back.

"Give him airrr, fer Gawd's sakes! You, cowboy . . . Back off . . ."

"I'm with him. We come outta' the station together. Somebody get a ambulance. His shoulder's busted. Maybe a fractured skull . . ."

"The ambulance is on its way," said the other cop. "The hospital's just up the street. Take it easy, mister. And keep your mitts off him."

"I ain' touchin' nothin'. Hey . . ." He confronted the gawking bystanders. "Anybody a doctor? He needs help bad . . ."

No doctors, no nurses. Only curious oglers fascinated by the sudden drama intruding into their dull lives. Within minutes an ambulance came clanging up. In the meantime four more policemen, including a sergeant, showed up. They made a pathway through the crowd. Two white-clad orderlies brought a stretcher. They eased the still-unconscious Olcott onto it. He was shoved into the ambulance like a pie into an oven. Bert confronted the man at the reins.

"I'm comin' with you."

"No, sir. It's against regulations."

"He's my brother. I'M COMIN'!"

"Okay, okay."

The ambulance pulled out. Bert took no notice of the pretty girl in the red and gray silk dress. With the outrageously large matching hat and even more outrageous-looking feather waving atop it.

Watching Bert, she herself failed to see the large, red-faced man approach the sergeant in charge. Who saluted him.

Seventeen

Dupont Street bisects Chinatown from California to Broadway. Two blocks wide from east to west on Sacramento, Clay, Commercial, Washington, Jackson, Pacific, and Broadway Streets. And from Kearney to Stockton, crossing Dupont. On every side, red and gilt assault the eye; for this is Canton or Shanghai or Hong Kong compressed and thrust into San Francisco. East surrounded by West.

Large signs with carved Chinese characters hang outside stores and shops. Every nook and corner along the sidewalks is crammed with the stalls of curbside merchants selling vegetables, fruits, and sweets. Skilled cobblers, tinkers, chair menders, razor sharpeners, and fortunetellers peddle their services. Barbers, jacks-of-all-trades, and those with little to sell but their glibness hawk their wares. Lacquered boxes, vases, and ivory carvings are displayed for sale. Tobacco, tea, dried fish, clothing, bottled essences, flowers, screens, scrolls, and paintings fill windows. Jade, opal, pearl, and intricately crafted, solid-gold jewelry can be had; rings, earrings, pins, pendants, figurines, and exquisite jade bead necklaces are available. Freshly roasted ducks, squabs, chickens, and suckling pigs hang in store windows.

Down a darkened alley one encounters the strange medicinal smell of an herbal apothecary. And upstairs through that window above the wrought-iron balcony one may see an acupuncturist practicing his ancient art: bloodlessly removing his patient's troublesome appendix. Not a basement, cellar, dormitory, loft, garret, or covered court is not teeming with humanity. Through the fog, the alleys, lanes, and byways give forth dense clouds of smoke from open cook fires. The housetops are white with drying garments and linens, fluttering from a network of clotheslines. A flurry of weird and alien music from clashing cymbals, flute, moon fiddle, and butterfly harp fills the air.

The buildings are of plain American architecture. But there the white man's influence begins and ends; for the theaters, restaurants, fan-tan parlors, and joss houses are distinctively oriental in appearance. Lit with lanterns of all sizes, shapes, and colors, fluttering, flickering, swinging in the breeze coming off the bay.

The Chinese are abroad in great numbers, milling through the streets and down the lanes and alleyways. Sitting before their doors, selling, buying, bartering, chatting, living out their narrow lives doggedly clinging to the ways of old China.

Down Dupont Street to Clay. Turn into Clay and immediately off into an alley: a dank and slimy passageway illuminated by a single lantern suspended twenty feet overhead. Barely revealing a scampering rat and four steps. Up the steps to a deep-set door painted bright red. A bronze knocker in the shape of a Foo dog is rapped. Twice. The muted padding of steps is heard. The door opens. The sickly-sweet odor of incense rushes to the nostrils. Down a narrow hallway over a faded runner depicting herons, larks, and peacocks. Pass between matching, threadbare, damask wall hangings to an amber bead curtain. Orange light from an unseen source glows feebly in the low-ceilinged room. Bare-board, two-tiered bunks line the walls on three sides. A teapot and empty cups are set out on an exquisitely engraved copper tray on a low, sandalwood table. But the men in the four bunks take no notice. They lie on their sides, faces toward their individual trays, heads resting on high, hard pillows fashioned of bamboo covered with leather. One, the youngest, takes his pipe in hand and with the other hand takes a dipper and places the sharp end of it into the treacly opium. Round and round he twists it. He gets a large drop to stick; he brings it to the

flame of his lamp and twirls it slowly, roasting it. It takes on
the appearance of burnt worsted.

He then gently heats the center of the bowl. In it there is a
small opening. He thrusts the end of the dipper into the
opening; he twirls it deftly and withdraws it. The opium is
left sticking to the bowl just above the opening.

He takes the stem of this pipe between his lips; he holds
the bowl over the lamp. Three times he inhales, swallowing
the smoke, holding it, exhaling through the mouth and nose.

A door leads out of the den; access to a number of rooms
in the rear. In one, lying on a narrow pallet, is Ben Slaughter.
Brought from the sidewalk in front of the Java Hotel to
Dupont Street. To the alleyway off Clay. Down the passageway, through the red door and the opium den to here. None of
which he had seen, thanks to the chloroform. He had come
to, his head aching furiously. His mouth was filled with the
nauseating taste of the drug; he had no idea where he was.

He tried to get up; the room whirled; he fell back grunting.
He called out, but the effort only intensified the throbbing.
The door opened. The face beneath the plain, black silk
coolie cap startled him. It was deathly pale with a strange,
gray-blue cast. The cheekbones were unusually high, the eyes
like black pearls. A slender, straight nose. An all but lipless
mouth that looked like a slit in a piece of canvas. The
questioning expression gave way to a frigid smile. Quickly on
and off.

"Awake at last."

"What is this? Who are you?"

The newcomer bent his full length Ming-style robe in a low
bow. Again he smiled, holding it in place longer.

"I am Kwan Ti. The name means nothing to you, but I
have the honor to be called after the great military hero of the
Three Kingdoms. The originator of the Chinese blood-brother
oath. Alas, the history of our beloved land is of little interest
to you, I am sure, Mr. Ahhh . . ."

Ben held the sides of his head; he lifted himself to a sitting
position. The pounding did not increase. He sucked his lungs
full of the stale air.

"You knock me out, drag me here, lock me up, and you don't even know who I am? My name is Slaughter."

"A pleasure to meet you, Mr. Slaughter. Your companion at the hotel was a Mr. Littlejohn, isn't that so?"

"Was. Why did you have to murder him? He was harmless, he . . ."

Up came Kwan Ti's hand stopping him. He closed the door behind him and approached.

"My men were overzealous in carrying out their orders. Their greatest desire is to please me. Sometimes they overdo it. They searched the room, failed to find the ruby. They became angry . . ." He spread his hands. "His answers to their questions failed to satisfy them."

He sat on the corner of the pallet. "The ruby is not on you, Mr. Slaughter. What have you done with it?"

"I've never had it."

"Not even back in St. Louis. And before?"

"I'm talking about since it was stolen."

"So Mr. Littlejohn was telling the truth. Mr. Olcott has it."

Ben studied his eyes. No sense lying to this one, he thought. What he doesn't know already he can easily guess. Fit together from what he already knows. Yes, Olcott had it. And Bert had Olcott.

Hopefully.

He nodded. "So you don't need me."

"Ah, but we do have you. Should we let you go? I think not. You may prove useful. I see by your expression that you do not understand what this is all about. Permit me to explain. The ruby is the prize of the collection of the king of Belgium, is that not so?"

"Yes."

"No, Mr. Slaughter. It does not belong to His Majesty. It never has. It is and always will be the property of the Chinese imperial family. Of Tsz'e Hsi, the dowager empress. The emperor Hien-feng, who died in eighteen sixty-five, had it before Her Majesty. He left the throne to his son, T'ung-chi, a child of five. Tsz'e Hsi rules in his stead.

"The ruby has a fascinating history. It is one of five

identical stones which form the Constellation of the Serpentfish. The five stones are priceless and any single one is considered as valuable as the group itself. Since its loss greatly diminishes the worth of the five together . . ."

"What does all this have to do with me? You know *I* don't have it."

"Ah, but perhaps you can lead us to it."

"I don't see how."

"Come now, Mr. Slaughter, ever since it was stolen you have been trying to recover it. Assigned by your superiors to. You and your estimable father."

Ben's mind picked up speed; spinning through the persistent throbbing. Straws invited grasping.

"I don't know where Olcott is. I don't know where my father . . ."

"They will arrive in San Francisco together this evening. They will be carrying the ruby." He got up. "Come with me, please. There is someone I wish you to meet. Are you feeling better? Does your head still ache?" He produced a pill as if from thin air. "Chew this, swallow it. It is remarkably efficacious. And completely harmless."

His hand placed lightly against Ben's back, he ushered him down the hallway to a door. He unlocked it. Two large lanterns spread yellow light throughout the little room. At the top of the rear wall was a large rectangular window. It was partially open. A muffled symphony of street sounds came through it. Two tables, a stool, and bed furnished the room. On the bed lay a man fully clothed. His head was massive: he was bald, deeply tanned, with a fringe of black hair surmounting his ears. Pince-nez were fastened to his coat lapel with a black silk ribbon and lay in the groove between his arm and side. His suit was linen, expensively tailored. He wore an immaculate white shirt, wing collars, and dark-blue tie. Gold cuff links showed below his cuffs. His hands were folded on his stomach. His well-polished, expensive-looking shoes had been removed and placed on the floor beside the bed. He was dead.

"This is Mr. Mortimer Fordyce-Molyneux. He has come from Sydney, Australia, for the express purpose of purchasing the ruby from Mr. Littlejohn and Mr. Olcott. For ransom. He intended to sell it back to the Belgians. Unfortunately, Mr. Fordyce-Molyneux knew nothing whatsoever of the ruby's history. And his plan involving Littlejohn and Olcott created a problem for us. When he arrived in this country we had no choice but to eliminate him.

"We've been awaiting the arrival of the collection here so that *we* could reclaim the ruby. How it got from Peking to Antwerp is a long story. One of duplicity and corruption I won't bore you with. But before it was stolen, it had been the property of the Chinese imperial family for nearly a thousand years. The Belgian's claim to it is entirely false.

"I tell you all this and introduce you to the late Mr. Fordyce-Molyneux so that you will appreciate the seriousness of our intentions. Mr. Littlejohn's death was regrettable, but ... Two men have already given their lives. Others, even you yourself, will also die. If it is necessary."

His coal-black eyes pierced Ben's. He smiled icily.

"We *will* recover what is rightfully ours."

• • • •

Bert stood talking to a doctor by the reception desk of the Central Emergency Hospital. The doctor was middle-aged, a portly man, harried and overworked-looking. Again and again his fist went to his mouth to stifle a yawn. His eyes were the color of unripe cherries from lack of sleep. He had jammed his stethoscope into the pocket of his white linen jacket. And after it his fist, clenching and unclenching it nervously.

"His shoulder is badly fractured: the clavicle, acromium, and coracoid. He's still out from the blow to his head, but it was glancing. There's no fracture there. It's hard to gauge the degree of concussion. I don't think it's terribly severe."

Nurses swished by on either side of them, the clicking of their heels rising to the vaulted ceiling. Echoing. Gas lamps illuminated the spacious reception area. Uncomfortable-looking straight-backed chairs lined the wall behind Bert on both sides of the entrance. The pudgy, wheat-blonde receptionist behind the desk ignored them. Her head was bowed to her work.

"Can I see him?" asked Bert.

"I just told you, he's unconscious."

"I just gotta ask him one question."

"Mr. . . ."

"Hume. He's my brother, Henry."

The doctor was unable to suppress a wry smile. He lowered his head and peered over his spectacles. "And I'm his sister. I'm afraid I don't see any family resemblance . . ."

"There's somethin' I got to know, Doc. I mean got to. The name o' the hotel we were on our way to when this all happened. He never did say. Ask him for me, will you? It's terrible important."

"You're not listening, Mr. Hume. He's unconscious. Why don't you take a seat over there and wait. He should come around in an hour or so. When he does I'll let you in to see him for a minute or so. Go ahead, sit down."

"But . . . '

The doctor smiled patronizingly. He nodded. "I'll see you later, I've got patients waiting . . ."

Off he went. Bert took a chair. Of all the stupid things to happen. The worst of it was Olcott never had gotten around to telling which hotel Littlejohn—and Ben—were waiting in. There had to be a hundred hostelries in the city. Wherever they'd ended up, Ben would be there. Had to be. He'd never let him out of his sight, unless he'd already gotten the Dragon's Eye away from him. That was possible.

Damn Olcott for not telling the name. Damn him for ducking under the scaffolding to get around the crowd. Damn, lousy, stinking, rotten luck! Damn, dumb plank coming down the very second he stepped out from under. At that, crazy as it was, why should it surprise him? Since St. Louis, practically everything had gone wrong.

He bit off a chaw of Red Bull. He was working on it when he noticed there were no spittoons about. He eyed the desk opposite. The receptionist was still bent over her work. A lonely-looking potted palm stood in the corner to his left. He went to it, turned his back on the desk, and deposited his strool. He nearly missed the lip of the pot. He spit out his chaw; he couldn't be bothered walking back and forth every time the urge to spit came on. He went back to his chair and got out his newspaper.

Nothing much was going on in San Francisco. Nothing even as newsworthy as the warmed-over report on the lack of progress in the search for the Dragon's Eye. A treaty had been signed between the United States and China; it restricted immigration of Chinese labor. A Baptist minister, one Isaac Kalloch, had announced that he was running for mayor. Bert turned the page. The lamp above his head flickered. He stared at the paper. A name leaped at his eyes.

Frank Littlejohn.

"A visitor to our fair city identified as Mr. Franklin Littlejohn was attacked and brutally murdered in his room at the Java Hotel last evening. The room was thoroughly ransacked. Edgar Manor, the clerk on duty at the time, was unable to give the police any information regarding Littlejohn's assailants. Mr. Manor is quoted as saying he saw no suspicious characters in the hotel lobby. It is believed that more than one individual entered the room. A tong hatchet was found on the floor. The police are investigating."

"Ben! Jeez!"

He jumped up and sat back down immediately. It drew the receptionist's eye. She stared briefly, then lowered her eyes to her work.

No mention of Ben in the item. Only the one body discovered. Had Ben shared the room with Littlejohn? Or was he in another? Was he even registered there? If so, had he been out at the time? Must have been. Had to have been. On the other hand, it was possible he'd never even come to town. Bert stiffened. He could have been waylaid back in Utah. Murdered, himself! There or between there and here. By who, Littlejohn? He didn't look the murdering sort, but then who did? Everybody had murder in him, somewhere down deep. He folded the paper and tossed it onto a chair three away from him.

Visitors were arriving. Single individuals, twos, threes. The receptionist put her work aside and began pulling cards from a small box-file. Picking them out and handing them to the people approaching her. They ascended the stairs to the right. Bert watched them. An orderly was coming down. He gripped the bannister, supporting himself; his other hand went to his head. He seemed dazed. The people going up gawked at him. Halfway down, Bert saw that his forehead was bleeding. When he reached the floor and started toward the reception desk, he staggered. His legs buckled. Bert rushed to him. The receptionist came running up, her hands fluttering nervously. The orderly sat on the floor staring at his blood-stained fingers.

"They knocked me out. Only a few minutes, but . . . when I came to he was gone." He gaped at the woman and then at Bert. "They took him . . ."

"Take it easy, Willard," said the receptionist. "Help me get him behind the desk to a chair," she said to Bert.

They sat him in a chair. Incoming visitors milled about the other side of the desk. They stared curiously. Willard's head appeared to clear. The bleeding was only superficial; it had stopped. He glanced at Bert.

"It was the fellow you brought in, Mr. . . . ."

"Oh my God! Which room?"

"Two-o-one . . ."

Away sprinted Bert. He raced up the stairs. The receptionist bawled after him.

"YOU   CAN'T   GO   UP   WITHOUT   A PAAAAAAAAAAASSSSSSS . . ."

He found 201. Olcott was gone, his bedclothes in wild disarray. Bert ran back down to the main floor. The orderly was standing. A nurse had bandaged his cut. Bert ignored the receptionist's glare.

"Who were they?"

"Three Chinese. Mean-looking buggers. One was seven feet tall, honest to God. Biggest man I've ever seen. He knocked me down. I hit my head. Passed out. Last thing I saw was him picking up the patient. Holding him like he was a baby, light as a feather. They came in the window off the fire escape. I was outside in the corridor. I heard a noise.

They were already in when I went back in. He, the big one, was behind the door. Behind me . . .''

Bert ran out the front door past more visitors coming in. He stopped on the sidewalk to mull the situation over. Two men came toward him, one beefy-faced, belligerent looking. He marched with his fists swinging at his sides. Bert didn't recognize him; he hadn't seen him earlier, coming up to the sergeant in charge at the scene of Olcott's accident. The man with him was also in plainclothes. He was a head and a half shorter. He wore handlebar mustaches so fastidiously kempt they appeared artificial. He hurried his step to keep up with the other. The bigger man strode up to Bert. He grabbed his arm.

"Slaughter . . .''

"Leggo o' me, ya big ape.'' Bert jerked loose. "Who are you?''

"Detective Gogarty. This here's Detective Swanson. Hand over the hardware, you're under arrest.'' He snatched out Bert's gun. "Let's go.''

"Wait a minute, what for?''

"It'll all be explained down at the station.''

Again he seized Bert's arm. Again he shook free. They closed in, one on either side of him.

"Let's go,'' said Gogarty.

Off they walked. They had spotted and collared him fast; neither saw the young woman coming up behind them. She wore an attractive red and gray dress. And an enormous hat with a large, dyed ostrich feather atop it. She stood hands on hips glaring after them. Two impressively large and expressionless Chinese stood watching with her.

Eighteen

Captain Powderly, in charge of the California Street Station, looked like Gogarty's older brother. He was as big and beefy, and affected an even more truculent expression. He sat backwards in his chair, sleeves rolled up, his muscular forearms crossed on top of the back. He sweat profusely; his nose dripped and he swiped at it with the back of one tobacco-yellowed finger.

The look on his face said that he did not like Bert. Seated opposite him, Bert did his level best to return the disfavor. The drab little room smelled of paint; neither it nor anything in it appeared newly painted, however. At the far end of the hall, two men were arguing heatedly. A third was laughing at them. The captain motioned Gogarty to close the door. He did, then resumed leaning against the wall by it. Swanson sat on the other side cleaning his fingernails with his fingernails.

The captain leveled what was intended to be an intimidating stare at Bert

"Where's your sidekick, cowboy?"

"Dunno. We been outta touch."

"Since . . ."

"Way back. Provo, Utah."

"You've found the ruby . . ."

"The devil I have. I'm lookin' for it."

"Your boss, Mr. Tevis, thinks you've found it. Cowboy."

"He's fulla' you know what. An' stop callin' me cowboy!"

"You're not a cowboy?"

"No."

"How come you wear that funny hat? Those funny boots? That hayseed get-up?"

"If I had the friggin' thing you think I'd be hangin' roun' that hospital waitin' for Olcott to come to?"

"So Olcott knows where it is."

"He keeps sayin' he does."

"He does, cowboy. Why else would they snatch him, eh?"

"How come *you* snatched me? On what charge? You sure can't hold me, you got nothin' . . ."

"We got suspicion. You look guilty to me, cowboy. Isn't he the guiltiest-looking hombre you boys ever saw? Hey, where's your lassoooo?"

"Up your nose, wiseguy. I'm leavin' . . ."

He started up. Gogarty pushed him down hard.

"You're going into the cage. Mr. Tevis's orders." Powderly leered.

"Bull! Lock up him, why don'tcha? He's looney as a squirrel in heat. He is. Talks to himself, thinks everybody's out to get him. He got you 'round his finger has he? That's it. Must be. I mean charge me for real, somethin' solid, or lemme walk. Get in touch with my chief, James B. Hume, why don'tcha? He'll straighten you out."

"I know James Hume."

"So go get him. Bring him in, he'll vouch for me. I dunno where the ruby is, but I'm bustin' my neck tryin' to find it. Why don't you boys just stay outta it? All you're doin' is messin' things up."

"Testy coot, aren't you? You always so irritable? Why don't we give you a nice, cool cell, bring your temperature down. Stick him in the old corral, Gogarty. Funny hat and all."

Bert cursed and lunged for him. Gogarty and Swanson grabbed him.

"You're makin' a big mistake. When this comes out in the wash you'll wind up lookin' like a buncha lame-headed greenhorns that screwed up proper. That's 'zactly what you're doin', you know."

"I know. Look at me, I'm worried sick. Where's your sidekick?"

"I already said. I don' know. You deaf? I know he's in trouble . . ."

"How do you know that?"

"He . . ."

He stopped. Why tell them anything? They were groping for bits and pieces. Obviously didn't know a thing. Level with them and they really would mess things up. Probably get Ben killed. Him, too. Damn Tevis! Damn suspicious old woman!

"Why don't you be smart and cooperate, cowboy?"

"Make it easy on myself, right? Who you bullin'? You're gonna lock me up if I don't talk or if I do. If I don', what'll you do, hang me?"

"Get him out of here!"

● ● ● ●

Down the hall past small offices left and right they marched him. Past the desk sergeant's station opposite the stairs leading down to the front door. Left through a door labeled *No Smoking*. Into the cell area. There were six individual cells lined up across from the drunk tank. The cop that locked him up looked no more than eighteen. His grin mask seemed pasted to his skinny head. He tittered with every other sentence. His Adam's apple was never still. He stuck him in a cage between two already occupied. He lowered his voice to describe Bert's neighbors. The crazy-eyed unshaven, disheveled-looking one on the left had been locked up for throwing vitriol at a city councilman. The one on the other side—big enough to go six rounds with Gogarty or the captain—was in for molesting a nine-year-old girl.

Bert ignored both. He lay on his cot; hands behind his head, he stared at the peeling ceiling. And lined up the events in chronological order. He then began inserting suppositions and conjecture into the skein.

"Gotta cigarette, soldier?" asked Vitriol.

Bert waved him away.

"He don' wanna be frans," said Molester.

Bert closed his eyes; he snored. Out front, the desk sergeant dozed over his half-finished game of solitaire. Down the hall, the captain, Gogarty, and Swanson discussed the "Wells Fargo Ruby Case." A woman came in the front door and asked about her husband. The sergeant poked through his desk file. He found the name and apprised her of the status of her husband's case.

Suddenly the double doors behind the woman burst open. In surged a crowd of Chinese clad in identical floppy blue pajamas, their hair bound in traditional queues. In seconds the doors became floodgates, a mass of orientals pouring into the station. In forty seconds hundreds filled every foot of space in the reception area and hall. They burst through into the cell area. They squeezed into the narrow way separating the holding tank from the cells. Crushed tightly, they jabbered in singsong voices. And waved bits of paper displaying Chinese characters.

Bert had jumped up. Men pressed against his door so tightly, once in place not one could move. A voice called to him through the barred window at his back.

"Mister . . ."

He turned. And gasped. A heavy chain was being wrapped around the six bars. He stared. The bars were ripped from their moorings as easily as if they'd been wooden sticks set in mud. Concrete dust rose in tiny puffs. A face filled the opening. A Chinese.

"You will come with us."

"In a pig's eye . . ."

A hand appeared alongside the face. In it a .45 aimed straight at him. A thumb cocked it.

"You come . . ."

He crossed to the window. Behind him the seething mass of men continued their jabbering. Out front at the far end of the hall, the captain and two detectives struggled to get out of the room. They pushed futilely against the mob. The woman visitor had taken refuge behind the desk with the sergeant. Grinning, babbling Chinese locked them in place on both sides. Upwards of a thousand men had piled into the station;

they filled every inch in the hall, the reception area, and the
walkway separating the cells and the holding tank.

Bert stood under the now barless window. The biggest
hands he had ever seen reached down and pulled him
upward and through, as easily as if he'd been a rag doll. He
found himself standing in an alleyway surrounded by Chinese.

"What . . ."

The one word was all he got out. He was grabbed from
behind, his arms securely pinned. He was quickly gagged and
his wrists and ankles bound with wire. The man who had
pulled him from the cell towered seven feet. His shoulders
were massive, his bare biceps enormous and glistening with
sweat. He picked Bert up and carried him across his forearms. As a maid would carry bed sheets and towels. As
lightly. As easily.

Nineteen

So sweet was the smell of the incense, Bert felt his stomach tug with nausea. Kwan Ti had introduced himself and immediately apologized for the odor. He explained that the incense was burnt continuously to mask the even more distasteful odor of the *ah pin yin* being roasted and smoked in the den in the front of the house.

"I shall not bore you with trivial conversation." Kwan Ti held out his hand. "The ruby, please."

"I don' have it. I coulda' tol' your highbinder pals, only they didn' give me a chance."

"I see. You prefer to be persuaded. Your friend, Mr. Olcott, made the same choice. Unfortunately for him. He was placed in a room quite like this one. Two of my men who are very skilled in the art of torture tried to induce him to talk. They used slender steel needles about eight inches long. They are thrust into the body's natural apertures and expertly manipulated. I could not bring myself to stay and watch. The screaming is always intolerable, the agony . . . Before he died, Mr. Olcott disclosed that *you* have the ruby."

"He's a friggin' liar!"

"You swallowed it."

"I never . . ."

"My men inform me that he insisted you did. He repeated it over and over. Would a man facing certain death lie? What

143

would he hope to gain, time? I think not. I believe he was telling the truth. You swallowed the ruby.''

"I didn'. I never laid a hand on it. Oh, I seen it, but that was before. Before it was stolen. He was talkin' through his hat. That's the god's honest truth."

"Would you care to see the late Mr. Olcott?"

"I'll pass."

"Pity. The expression fixed on his face in his death agony is indescribable. Fascinating. Would you care to see your son?"

"You mangy scum! Whatja do to him?" He jumped up; he grabbed Kwan Ti's robe front. "TALK! TELL ME!"

With an upward thrust and quick sideward movement of his arms, Kwan Ti easily broke the hold.

"Calm yourself, Mr. Slaughter. Your son is unharmed. I shall bring him to you; you may see for yourself. You shall have a chance to talk privately. Five minutes. If, at the end of that time, you still refuse to disclose the ruby's whereabouts, you will both die. Do you understand?"

"I didn' swallow the friggin' thing . . ."

Kwan Ti went out. Seconds later Ben was pushed into the room and the door shut. From the other side came Kwan Ti's voice.

"Five minutes."

Bert threw his arms around Ben. "You okay?"

"Okay. You?"

"Aces."

"How's the operation?"

"Okay. Never mind that. Did you see Olcott?"

Ben sat staring at the floor. His shoulders slumped. His voice and posture were a portrait of despair.

"I didn't need to. *I heard him die*. I never want to hear anything like that again as long as I live. They stuck me in the room next door. It was ghastly. I broke out in a sweat just listening." He held out his shaking hand.

"Poor fella . . ."

"What are we going to do, Bert?"

"You're askin' me?"

"We've got about three minutes."

"Take it easy. He's not gonna kill neither of us. He killed Olcott an' come up deuces. He's sure not gonna kill us. We're his last chance to find the thing. Who is he, anyhow? How'd he an' his highbinder pals get into this?"

"It's a long story. Let's save it till later. If there is a later."

"I can't believe that son of a gun Olcott, lyin' like that."

"He's dead; he died suffering horribly."

"He's still a damned liar! He tol' that slant-eyed scum I swallowed the Dragon's Eye. You ever hear such nonsense?"

"Wait a minute . . ."

"Facin' death an' he lies in his teeth. How do you figger that? Is that crazy?"

"That wasn't what he said."

"Was, too. That chink was just in here . . ."

"He didn't. I heard him. What he said was *it's in his stomach.*"

"*He* tol' me Olcott said I swallowed it."

"That's probably what his men told him. Everyone here except him speaks broken English. To them, *swallowed is the same as in the stomach.* Which it is, broadly speaking."

"What are you talkin' about?"

Ben's eyes had come alive. He swung a hand in the air, his finger pointing. Gesturing, pushing his point home. He started to answer when gunfire sounded deafeningly loud outside the door. Wood splintered and shattered. Men yelled in high-pitched voices. Gunshots. Cursing. Doors slamming. Yelling. Roaring. Men rushing about. Bert jerked open the door.

"It's the cops!" Ben roared triumphantly.

"Let's get outta' here . . ."

"Why? They're rescuing us. They're saving our lives . . ."

"We don' need 'em anymore than this buncha' chopstick benders. How do we get outta' this dive?"

"Follow me . . ."

They ran down the hall to the room occupied by Fordyce-Molyneux's corpse. The door was locked. An ax bit through the outer door set at right angles to the door facing them. Somebody on the other side of the axed door was kicking at the lock. It bent outward, but did not snap. Again the ax ripped the paneling. Bert and Ben shouldered the door to the room. The lock shattered. In they rushed, slamming the door behind them.

Fordyce-Molyneux lay stonelike and staring.

"This boy doesn' look too good..."

"Never mind him. I'll fill you in on everything later. Let's get out of here."

The police broke through the back door. In they boiled, shouting and firing their pistols. The firing stopped, but the shouting, scrambling about, and slamming of doors went on. Ben pulled the bed under the partially opened window. He stood on the bedstead. He pulled himself up and through the window. And reached back down.

"Grab hold. Careful of your stitches..."

He pulled Bert up. Bert grabbed the sill and squirmed through. Cursing every inch of the way. Outside they ran. Down the alley into the brightly lit street. Down the street toward the docks. They ran and ran. Bert struggled to keep up. Through mobs of pedestrians, dashing in front of oncoming carriages and wagons. Running. Running...

"We're in the clear, for Godsakes. Slow down...BEN!"

They stopped by a lamppost. They dropped onto the curb; both panting furiously.

"You...o...kay?" Ben asked.

Bert could not answer. Only nod. He fought to catch his breath. His hand stole to his side. They had reached an area of little traffic. Up the block, a man and woman stood talking in a doorway. An empty, flat-topped brougham clattered by.

"I'm...o...kay."

"I've figured it out, Bert. I have..."

"What?"

"The Dragon's Eye. It's in your incision."

"Bull!"

"It is. It's got to be!"

"You're nuts. Whatcha been eatin', opium? You're dreamin'..."

"Don't talk, just listen. Go back to Gypsum. You didn't

find the ruby on either when you searched them. You went into the saloon. The woman . . ."

"Bedelia Strump. She was kinda' tasty . . ."

"She comes up to you. She starts drinking with you. She slips something into your glass. You come down with violent cramps. The next thing you know you're flat on your back. A doctor is giving you chloroform. You wake up minus your appendix. With the ruby inside you."

"Bull. In spades!"

"I'm not finished. From that point on, Littlejohn and Olcott do everything humanly possible to stay close to you. After running like rabbits for two days and nights trying to get away, they do a complete turnabout."

"Ben . . ."

"Let me finish. They board the train; we follow. All four of us survive the wreck. The stage is held up."

"Cutler. Rotten scum . . ."

"You chase him two hundred miles. Almost to the Arizona border. *He* catches *you*. Only who pops up? Who steps in and saves your life?"

"That was jus' a dumb coincidence."

"Some coincidence. Two hundred miles long . . ."

"Hold your horses. That doc he took me to in Orton. I remember he asked who took my 'pendix out. I tol' him Doctor Fizzle. Olcott butted in. He said Friz . . . Then stopped real quick. The guy's name was Frizzell. How could Olcott know that?"

"Unless he'd been doing business with him."

"They coulda' known each other before Olcott even come to town. Frizzell an' her could be the reasons him an' Littlejohn did!"

"They were let out of jail at eight the next morning. They left town. So Marshal Butz told you. But let's go back to Ebenezer Canyon, you and Cutler and Olcott. That, Bert, is the clincher. You see, don't you?"

"I guess . . ."

"Olcott followed you every step of the way down. He knew it would come to a showdown. He didn't want anything to happen to you. As things turned out he saved your life.

Saved the life of the man who was going to put him behind bars. How chivalrous of him.''

'' 'Cause he *had* to.''

"Eureka!" Ben beamed victoriously. He raised his fist and shook it.

"He give me his iron when mine got ruined.''

"And let you think you were escorting him all the way out here.''

"I did. I had the gun, didn' I?''

"He planned to get you to the Java Hotel. Once he got you there he'd turn the tables on you. On us. Get rid of me, tie you down, open you up . . .''

"An' dig out the stone.''

"Exactly.''

"I still don' b'lieve it. It's wild. . . .''

"Let's see if I'm right.''

"Cut me open again? Jeez, I should have friggin' buttons sewed on there. It gets opened an' closed like a snap-top purse. No, thanks. Not again.''

Ben slipped an arm around his shoulders. "It's in there, Bert. It's got to come out. Let's go find a bed for the night. Tomorrow morning we'll find us a surgeon. The real thing, no vet.''

"Jeez! Why the devil does this have to happen to me? Every time. Why me?''

Into a long, windy, repetitive diatribe he flew. Bemoaning and bewailing his luck, in the vulgarest terms imaginable. He castigated the Fates, Wells Fargo, Lloyd Tevis, Bedelia Strump, Littlejohn, and Olcott. He dressed down his kidnappers, China in general, the Chinese love of immigration, his life, the world. Ben listened. He did feel sorry for him, but had to battle back laughter. And did so until his stomach ached.

Bert finally talked himself out; they got up from the curb and went looking for a hotel.

Twenty

"Police Raid Headquarters of Notorious See Yup Tong

The Chinatown squad joined forces with officers from the California Street Station last night in a lightning raid on See Yup Tong headquarters in Peach Blossom Alley off Clay Street. Twenty-four Celestials were arrested and booked on various charges, ranging from opium smoking to carrying concealed weapons. The prize catch was Kwan Ti, reputed leader of the See Yups. The bodies of two white men were found on the premises. According to the police report, one of them had been subjected to torture. Neither corpse has as yet been identified. The prisoners are being held in the California Street Station pending arraignment.

Two Wells Fargo detectives are also being sought in connection with the theft of a priceless ruby, part of the collection of the Belgian royal family. Both men were believed to be prisoners of the See Yups, but a thorough search conducted by the police failed to find either man. Mr. Lloyd Tevis, president and chief executive officer of Wells Fargo, refused to answer questions posed by reporters regarding a possible connection between the See Yups and the

detectives. Both had originally been assigned to guard
the collection during its U.S. tour.''

Bert slammed the newspaper into the trash basket.

"This is it," said Ben, indicating a small wooden sign at
the side of a large, green, windowless door. "E.B. Abramowitz,
Surgeon.''

"You think I'm gonna walk in on him, strip down, an' let
him cut me open, somebody I never even laid eyes on b'fore?
You gotta be kiddin' . . .''

"We've been all through that, we decided.''

"You, not me. It's not your gut he's gonna be pokin' into.
How would you like some stranger rootin' 'round inside o'
you, pickin' an' pokin', lookin' for what prob'ly isn't even
there? That part o' me has been so abused, so beat on an'
ripped up an' dug into an' out it's a wonder it's still
alive. Which it's prob'ly not; it's sure never gonna heal, not
proper . . .''

Ben pulled open the door. "You're afraid, right?''

"WHAT KINDA' STUPID THING IS THAT TO SAY?
After the life I've led? What I've gone through? You think
there's anythin' in the worl' I'm afraid of? 'Fraid's the
furthest thing from my mind; it's this constan' cuttin' an'
tearin' an' stitchin' o' my poor defenseless flesh!''

"Up the stairs, my ears are starting to ring.''

● ● ● ●

Enoch Abramowitz was young, bright eyes, bright looking,
every inch the doctor. At first glance. Unlike the doctors in
the hinterlands, he did not work in rolled-up shirt sleeves and
vest. With cigar in mouth and ashes falling on the patient. He
wore a pristine white jacket that buttoned up to his left
shoulder. He introduced his nurse as Miss Ridgley. She wore
a starched, black cotton uniform. With a little pleated white
cap with a black ribbon circling the top.

The doctor's reception room was walled by three bookcases.
They were crammed with medical tomes from floor to ceiling.
His examination-operating room was immaculate; as neat as

the proverbial pin; steel and glass and porcelain in shining array.

He looked like a man not easily astonished. Then Ben explained their problem. Abramowitz's soft brown eyes widened; he sat straight up in his chair.

"Are you serious? It's a little early in the day . . ."

"I know it sounds far-fetched. Let me explain."

"I will," said Bert. "These two owlhoots I was chasin' through Kansas got tired o' runnin' an' turned the tables on me. Secretlike. Got this woman to drug me; I come down with cramps so fierce my stomach like to exploded. I was helpless; they operated on me, took my 'pendix out, stuck the ruby in. It's in there now. It's gotta come out. So *he* says . . ."

"Don't *you* want it out?"

"Do you have to cut? Couldn' you give me some castoria or Earlin' Fig Laxative? Let Nature take its course?"

"Mr. . . . , Hume was it?"

"That's right, this here's Mr. Ah . . ."

The doctor grinned. "Slaughter." Bert scowled; he snapped a glance at Ben seated beside him. Abramowitz nodded. "Fellows, I read the papers. Don't worry, I won't tattle on you. I've troubles enough of my own without getting involved in other people's. I won't know a thing if the police come snooping around.

"I was about to say, Mr. . . . Hume, from what you've told me the ruby is in your stomach wall. Not your intestine. I'm afraid a laxative just won't do the job. I don't have my first appointment until ten-thirty. It's now only a little after eight-thirty. Plenty of time; what do you say, shall we start digging?"

Bert winced. "Do you have to put it like that?"

"Can I be present?" Ben asked.

"You won't get sick on us, will you?"

"No."

"You're welcome to watch. Miss Ridgley, will you start preparations?"

"Yeth, Doctor."

Bert sighed. "I don' b'lieve this. I come clear 'cross the

country. For what, to get carved up again. An' on a empty stomach . . ."

"Relax, it'll be a cinch. Like pulling a tooth . . ."

"Oh, Jeez, whatta you got to say that for? I purely hate havin' a tooth pulled. Hate dentists, hate doctors, but dentists worse. What I can't stand is when they jam their knee 'gainst your chest an' yank."

The doctor chuckled. "I promise I won't do that. Go in the dressing room. Take everything off. You'll find a johnny shirt on a hook. Put it on backside to. We'll start in about ten minutes."

He beamed and rubbed his hands briskly. "This is going to be fun. I could wind up with a paragraph or two in *The Journal of Medicine*!"

Bert had paused with his hand on the doorknob. He turned; his eyes shriveled Abramowitz, but he said nothing.

•　•　•　•

Ben stood at the foot of the operating table. He wore a gauze mask. He exhaled forcefully through it, driving away the stink of the chloroform. Bert was under. The area was exposed and wiped with thimerosal by Nurse Ridgley. The doctor picked up his scalpel. He examined it, he raised it. Down it came. The instant it touched, a lump of nausea the size of his fist blossomed in Ben's stomach. He gagged. He covered his mouth. He lurched away to the bathroom.

•　•　•　•

Ben sat in the reception room. His stomach had settled; his color had come back. His impatience mounted. He glanced at the clock on the doctor's desk for the eighth time in the last two minutes. Four before nine. The door opened. Abramowitz grinned as he stripped off his gloves.

"All done. You feeling better?"

"How is he?"

"Hundred percent. He's tough as a mule. We moved him

into the rear room. He can recuperate there. He should stay overnight at least.''

"The ruby?''

Abramowitz's brow furrowed. "I looked for it. All around inside. I was very thorough . . .''

"You didn't find it!'' Ben shot to his feet. "That's impossible!''

The doctor stood aside. Nurse Ridgley appeared. She held a small packet of gauze in the crook of her arm. As if unfolding a blanket to reveal a baby, she showed him the Dragon's Eye. Ben's shoulders sagged in relief. He took it from her, gauze and all. He thanked her and Abramowitz profusely.

"How much do I owe you, Doctor?''

"Isn't the reward ten thousand?'' He laughed lightly. "My customary fee for an appendectomy without complications is twelve-fifty. But this was really a snap. I had my work cut out for me. Ha ha. Why don't we say ten bucks even? Plus corroboration in writing from you that I actually did remove a man's ruby. You know, for *The Journal of Medicine*. We doctors have to seize little nuggets of recognition when and where we can, you know.''

• • • •

"Gimme it.''

"It's all right, I'll hang onto it.''

"Give it here, Ben. I want it in my hand. I carried the damn thing fifteen hunnert miles in my gut, the least you can do is let me keep it.'' Ben handed him the Dragon's Eye. Bert held it up. "Pretty, ain't she? Shines like glass. Get my duds, we're gettin' outta' here.''

"You're not going anywhere. Doctor's orders. He wants you to stay overnight at least.''

"The devil with that. I'm sewed back up, bandaged, fit as a fiddle.'' He started up from the bed. He scowled, bit his lip, and sank back.

"Good. Excellent. I'll go out and get us some breakfast. Be back in half an hour.''

• • • •

He returned to find Bert sitting up. He grinned victoriously
through his discomfort. They shared a bottle of milk and fried
egg sandwiches.

"What's the next move?" Ben asked.

"I got it all figgered. You get over to Halleck an' Sansone
to the main office. Stan' 'cross the street from the front door.
When you see Hume come out for lunch, grab him. I'll be
downstairs waitin' in a doorway 'cross the street from here.
Bring him straight to me. Whatever you do, don' go up to his
office. Don' even go near the front door. If Tevis spots you,
you'll be a dead duck."

"If the cops spot *you*, you'll be back in jail. Bert, stay
away from California Street. Your friend Powderly has every
man under his command out looking for you by now. Your
clothes are a dead giveaway. Whatever you do, stay away
from California Street. Don't go near Chinatown."

"Whatta I look like, a idjit?"

• • • •

Lloyd Tevis was no longer the mass of quivering purple
outrage he had displayed in recent days. But his determina-
tion to "make the Slaughters pay in hard coin for the
humiliation their bungling has caused the company" was
unabating. He summoned James B. Hume to his office. Tevis
sat at his pier-table desk. A slender trail of smoke rose from
the ash of his Old Judge cigarette. His eyes betrayed a glint of
dudgeon, the residue of his last outburst the day before.

"I asked you in here to get your opinion of this disgusting
fiasco."

"I thought I'd already made that clear, sir."

"Have a chair, Jim. Smoke if you like."

Hume did not. He sat and looked past Tevis at a framed
autographed photograph of President Grant. Unconditional
Surrender looked disarmingly placid and amiable. Quite unlike his mood at the moment, reflected Hume.

"Jim, you can't be serious about resigning. Let me finish. I can understand your loyalty toward them. But to be frank, I think it's misplaced."

"Mr. Tevis, if they recover the ruby and return it. . . . And I haven't the slightest doubt but that they will . . . Won't that satisfy you that they haven't turned?"

"If they do return it, it could be because they've changed their minds. Decided the potato's too hot to handle."

He always had to seize on the black alternative, mused Hume. In his court, every man was guilty until proven innocent, not the other way around.

Tevis went on. "They've botched this thing from day one. Made an unholy mess, a complete disaster out of a routine assignment."

"Routine?"

"Routine. It was as far as St. Louis. They had the jewels under lock and key in a moving train. Armed, alert, fully prepared to defend them. The outlaws snatched the jewels right out from under their noses. They might as well have been fast asleep for all the resistance they put up.

"How many full-timers do we have on the detective payroll?"

"One hundred sixteen."

"This case will stand as an object lesson for a hundred and fourteen of them. The message should be abundantly clear: do your job, carry out your assignment to the best of your ability or suffer the consequences."

"That's unfair!"

"Sit down, Jim. You mean *I'm* unfair."

"I think so. I've thought it all along."

Tevis studied him for a long moment before resuming. He seemed to be searching Hume's thoughts. Picking through them. Recognizing loyalty, trust, and respect born of a long and fruitful association.

"I wish you'd reconsider. I can't accept your resignation. You're indispensable. Irreplaceable. I ask you as a friend, don't let your feelings hamstring your good judgment."

I could say the same to you, thought Hume.

"Sir, when the ruby's returned, the president will be satisfied, I'm sure. The company'll be in the clear. Suffering no ill effects. The Slaughters won't need to be fired. There'll be no reason to bring charges against . . ."

"You're asking me for a *quid pro quo*? You won't resign if I forgive and forget? I'm sorry, Jim. I don't make deals; my conscience doesn't permit it."

"As you wish. You have my resignation. As I said in my letter, I'll stay on till you can find a replacement."

"I appreciate it. Have a nice day, Jim."

•   •   •   •

Ten minutes after Ben left to get James Hume, Bert was up, dressed, and ready to leave. Doctor Abramowitz had gone to Central Emergency Hospital to see a patient. Nurse Ridgley tried to stop Bert from leaving.

"Doctor Abramowith thaid you're to thtay in bed!"

"I got things to do, missy. Tell him thanks for everythin'."

"Very well. Be pigheaded!" She seethed. She stamped her foot. "Thee here, I'm ordering you to thtay in bed!"

She was about five feet one. She probably weighed 104 carrying the watch at her lapel. Bert measured her up and down. She was pretty, but at the moment on fire. She ground her hips with her tiny fists; her chin jutted forth absurdly; her eyes smoldered.

"You're sore . . ."

"I'm telling on you! Doctor Abramowith will be very very angry. I'm VERY VERY ANGRY!"

"Take a pill, you'll feel better."

•   •   •   •

Out on the sidewalk he paused. His knees felt watery; he trembled slightly. He braced himself against the building, got his balance and his bearings, and crossed the street to the doorway of a small antique shop. It was closed, the door curtain drawn. Ben would not have approved of his getting up so soon. Anymore than did Nurse Ridgley. But he'd be damned if he'd have Hume show up at his bedside. If he ever found out that he'd been carrying the ruby in him all this time, Hume'd never let him forget it. Nor would Tevis. Or anybody else with the company. The newspapers would make him a laughingstock.

Abramowitz and the nurse wouldn't say anything. Any admission on the doctor's part that he was involved would only lead to embarrassing questions. The last thing he needed was publicity with a yellow taint. Later on, when it all died down, he could beat his drum as hard as he pleased in *The Journal of Medicine*. Beat his drum and blow his bugle. If he wanted. Not now, not with everything still up in the air. And threatening to come crashing down.

He spotted two policemen, crossed the street at the corner. They swung their sticks; they prattled away like two gossipy old maids. Both looked in his direction, then away. And disappeared behind the corner. Between it and the antique shop stood the Bush Street Theater and three stores. Just past the theater was the Bush Street Theatrical Costume & Supply Shop. He walked by the theater and the shop and was almost to the corner when an idea struck him. He stopped and turned around.

A jewel of an idea!

Twenty-one

"You're a card, cowboy, I swear. A barrel of laughs." Captain Powderly slapped his knee and guffawed. Gogarty, Swanson, and the two uniformed policemen who had picked Bert up joined the laughter.

"That's some disguise. Opera hat, full-length cloak. You shoulda' got yourself a pair o' fawn shoes. It was your boots that give you away," said one of the officers.

"His face was what give him away," said the other. "That mustache, all them lines and seams like somebody worked him over with a jackknife."

Bert flared. "You're not exactly han'some Prince Charmin', jerkface!"

"Take it easy," said the captain. He winked and grinned. "Guess what's waiting for you? Your old cell. It's been mopped out and everything."

"You can't lock me up."

"Can't we? You want a charge? Something other than suspicion? How about jailbreaking?"

"I didn' an' you know it. It was that buncha' Chinamen busted me out. Hauled me through the window at gunpoint. Woulda' blown my head off if I didn' do like they said."

"All I know is when we finally got the place cleared out you were gone. And he didn't even say goodbye."

Gogarty and Swanson cackled.

"On your feet," said the captain.

"I'll get you for this, wisemouth!"

"Sure you will. You'll have me tarred and feathered and run out of town on a rail. I can't sleep nights thinking about it. Get him out of here."

"Where's my forty-five?"

"Locked up; what do you think we do with evidence around here? Gogarty . . ."

Gogarty took hold of Bert's arm. He shook loose. The two detectives escorted him down the hallway. He carried his newly purchased cloak over his arm. His opera hat on his head. The desk sergeant smirked as they passed.

"Shut up!"

The front door opened. In strode Ben and James Hume. The captain was standing in his office doorway. He recognized the chief and came hurrying up.

"Mr. Hume, sir."

"Captain. Ben, this is Captain Powderly. Ben Slaughter, Earl."

"So you're his son, are you?"

"These jerks are tryin' to lock me up, Chief. Tell 'em who I am. Tell 'em they're making the bigges' mistake o' their worthless lives! You 'specially . . ." He glared at the captain.

"Why don't we all go back to my office and talk this over?"

Into the little office all six trooped. Joining the two arresting officers still lingering there.

"Are you okay?" Ben asked Bert.

"I was till those two flatfeet grabbed me."

"What's with the opera hat and cloak?"

The captain laughed. "He was trying to disguise himself. He looked ridiculous. Ask the boys here. All he did was draw attention to himself."

"He sure did," said one of the cops.

He nodded vigorously and smirked. Bert impaled him with a glare.

"Captain," said Hume, "I'd like you to release him in my custody."

Powderly sobered. "I don't know as I can, sir. Your boss, Mr. Tevis..."

"He'll know all about it. I'll assume full responsibility."

"He broke jail."

"I didn' no sucha thing!"

"Egbert." Hume eyed him wearily.

"I didn'!"

"He still refuses to give us any information," said the captain. "We haven't found the ruby. That's the main reason we're holding him. He may not have stolen it, but he's a material witness."

"You want it, why don'tcha come right out an' ask for it!"

Ben laid a hand on his arm. "Bert..."

Bert shook him off. "You get your ruby an' I get to walk, is that it?"

"Just one minute!" Hume made as if to step between them.

"Is that it, Powderly?"

"*Captain Powderly,* cowboy. Hand it over."

"Captain, Bert, oh, Lord..."

Ben went silently wild with frustration as Bert produced the stone. It was still in the gauze given him by Nurse Ridgley. He held it up. Ooohs and ahhhs and whews and wows arose.

"Is she a beauty?"

Powderly snatched it from him. Hume's shoulders sagged in defeat. Ben rolled his eyes and covered his face with one hand. The captain held the ruby up for all to see. He shook his head.

"Looks like red glass to me."

"Scratch it, wisemouth, an' they'll bury you in red glass. Lock you up for willful destruction of a million-dollar, priceless ruby. Prob'ly the mos' valuable in the whole, entire worl'. Ben, Chief, you two are witnesses I handed it over. You're responsible for it from now on, *Captain*. Now, gimme back my gun."

The tag was removed from Bert's pistol, formerly Henry Olcott's. The gun was returned.

"I really shouldn't be letting you go," said the captain.

"You goin' back on your word? You hear that, Chief, Ben? He's goin' back..."

"I do have to hold you accountable," said the captain.

Hume nodded. "I said I'd take responsibility, didn't I? You know where to find me if you need me. Egbert, Benjamin, let's get out of here."

• • • •

On the sidewalk Ben and Hume exploded in unison.

"I don't believe it!" Hume crimsoned and seethed. "I DON'T BELIEVE IT!"

"How could you blithely hand it over to him of all people!" said Ben. "He'll get all the credit. Wells Fargo'll get nothing. We'll get a ticket out of town. How could you do such a stupid thing?"

"You've ruined everything!" said Hume. "You two are the big losers."

On walked Bert. Slowly. Wordlessly. One on either side heaped insults, accusations, and criticism upon him. He reached the corner. He stopped and lowered himself slowly, somewhat uncomfortably to the curb.

"Get up!" Hume glowered.

"ON YOUR FEET!" Ben bellowed.

He ignored both. He had clamped his lips in a manner that suggested he was battling back the urge to respond. A grin was kindling; it gradually blossomed into a mischievous smile. Up came one finger. They fell silent. Bert slowly lifted his left leg over his right. He took off his boot. He tipped it down.

Out rolled the Dragon's Eye.

Ben gaped. Hume gasped and looked as if a thousand volts were coursing through him.

"By the Lord Harry!"

"Rec'nize it, son? Look familiar? It's the real thing." He shook his head. "My, but you surprised me back there. Dis'pointed me. You saw red, but not the right red, right? That hunk o' red glass I give Captain Loudmouth was just about the same color red this is. About the same size. But different cut. You jus' didn' look close 'nough to see, did you? If you did you'da seen that that there looks 'bout as much like this here as U.S. Grant looks like Lola Montez.''

"I didn't . . ."

"Look. You were too busy rilin' yourself up to explode. Rushin' up one side o' me an' down the other. An' you covered your eyes to boot . . ."

Hume's tone was apologetic. "Egbert, we both assumed . . ."

"Jumped to conclusions is what you did. Took it for granted I'd cave in under pressure. As if I would . . ."

Ben continued, stunned and staring. "What was that you gave Powderly? Where did you get it?''

"I thought you'd never ask. I spotted a theater costume store 'cross the street from the d . . .'' His eyes flashed to Hume and he caught himself. "On Bush Street. I'd already seen two cops an' I figgered when you two showed up we wouldn't get two blocks before somebody picked me up.

"Then it come to me. *Why not get myself picked up?* Delib'rate. Jump in the pot, ruin the stew, jump out again? Get the police off our backs permanent? An' what would? The Dragon's Eye, what else? I knew when you come back an' didn' find me you'd figger I got picked up, right? An' you had to know where they'd take me. An' they did. An' you come.''

"Where did you get the phoney?'' asked Hume.

"At the store, whatta ya think? I wasn' inside two shakes before I spotted a whole rack fulla' all kinds o' belts an' sashes an' such, a lot with make believe jewels. My eye went right to a big gold belt with fake rubies an' em'ralds an' sapphires clear 'round it. I bought it. I ran out the back, got outside, pried the biggest red one outta' its clamps, threw the belt in the trash, went back in an' bought the opry hat an' cloak. A secon' rate disguise to do 'zactly what Captain Loudmouth said . . .''

"Draw attention to yourself.''

"Right. Marched straight over to California Street. Got myself arrested.''

Hume glanced at Ben. "Incredible.''

"Nothin' credible about it. Just horse sense. Slaughter

brains put to work an' comin' up with a foolproof plan that worked out beautiful. As you both saw. Think about it, Captain Loudmouth never had seen the real Dragon's Eye. Wouldn't know it if it jumped up an' bit him. He was so eager to get his hands on it I coulda' handed him a painted walnut. Stupid idjit.''

Hume frowned. ''He'll be after you with a shotgun when he finds out you've tricked him. He'll be the laughingstock of the department.''

''Serve him right.''

Again Bert held up the ruby. ''Isn' she somethin' though? You can see why she's the apple o' King Leopole's eye.''

''Let me have it,'' said Hume. He stretched forth his hand.

Bert shook his head. ''Sorry, I can't. Not yet. Me an' Ben are on the pan; we gotta get off. I give this to you, you'll give it to Tevis. He'll give it to the ambassador or whoever. He'll wind up a hero; Ben and me'll wind up on the trash heap. You'll get it alright, I promise. Only not right away.''

''When?''

''Tomorrow mornin'. Nine o'clock in your office. You can tell Tevis if you want.'' He put his boot back on. He got up and dusted off his seat. ''We'll see you then.'' He flipped the ruby and caught it. ''Come on, Ben. We gotta find us someplace to hole up till tomorrow mornin'.''

''Lead on, oh wise and peerless master . . .''

''Good boy. You see how my son respects me, Hume?''

Twenty-two

News of the ruby's recovery swept through the city like fire through a dry woods. Kwan Ti's claim to it in the name of the imperial family proved to be poppycock. "So much hogwash strained through a oat sieve," as Bert phrased it. No less than three well-respected authorities on Chinese history and culture attested to it.

Captain Powderly was in luck. He averted the snare of humiliation Bert had so cleverly set for him. He was placing the "Dragon's Eye" in his safe file to await the arrival of the secret service men when it slipped from his fingers. It shattered. He nearly had a heart attack. He promptly realized he had been duped; he swore on his mother's grave that he would beat Bert Slaughter to death if he ever bumped into him again.

Lloyd Tevis arrived for work Wednesday morning. He immediately summoned Chief Hume to his office. Hume informed him that the Slaughters would be showing up at nine o'clock.

"Five minutes from now," he said. He stumped out his first La Flor de Portuondo, Chicos of the day. "With the ruby."

"You've seen them?"

Hume cleared his throat somewhat nervously. He was not accustomed to lying. It made him uncomfortable. But at the moment he appeared to have no alternative.

"Benjamin contacted me."

"Then you haven't actually seen the ruby."

"I have, sir. It's the genuine article, all right."

Tevis dropped into his chair like a half-filled sack of meal. He drew a gargantuan breath of relief.

"Thank God in heaven."

"Thank Egbert and Benjamin."

Tevis grunted. "You realize this doesn't change anything. They're still washed up with Wells Fargo. And I still plan to consult the lawyers in regard to bringing charges. This fiasco has taken years off all our lives. And we've them to thank."

Hume said nothing. Tevis wanted him to speak; he could feel it. To agree or argue. To say anything that would prolong the conversation. He'd be damned if he'd oblige him.

"Did either offer any explanation? Any excuse for their actions? I should say inactions . . ."

"They'll tell us the whole story, I'm sure."

"I can't wait. It should be priceless. That man is incorrigible. One hundred percent cock and bull. By comparison Ananias was a rank amateur."

Hume sighed inwardly. He wished the morning was over. He had no great, compelling urge to resign. Tevis hadn't knuckled under to his threat; he hadn't expected he would. But he'd made it and was stuck with it. And glad of it, deep down. A man had to stand on his hind legs once in awhile; definitely, when a principle was at stake. As it was in this.

A light tapping at the door. It opened and Tevis's secretary stuck her head in. She excused the interruption.

"The Slaughters are here, sir."

"Show them in."

"I don't know if I can. They're down in the lobby."

"Tell them to come up."

"They . . . It's . . . Perhaps you'd better come see for yourself, sir."

Tevis and Hume exchanged questioning glances. Hume followed him out and down the hallways. To the landing overlooking the lobby.

• • • •

Twenty-four reporters, six photographers and eighteen free-lance journalists crowded around Bert. The lobby was filled almost as snugly as the Chinese filled the California Street Station House two nights earlier. Ben stood at the rear of the crowd. Willingly yielding the spotlight to his father. Every office door on the main floor stood open. Clerks and secretaries filled the doorways to watch.

A reporter and photographer from *The Morning Call* were present; *The Examiner, The Bulletin, The Chronicle, The Evening Post,* the German language *California Demokrat,* and two men from the respected literary weekly *The Argonaut* were present. Representatives from the *Los Angeles Times, Saturday Time, Weekly Mirror, Herald* and *Express* had also come to town. Stringers covered the event for the *Morning Oregonian,* the *Oregon Daily Journal,* the *Evening Telegram,* the *Seattle Post Intelligencer,* the *Times* and assorted other West Coast dailies and weeklies.

"Show us the rock!

"Let's see it!

"Let's have a look!

"Hold it up for the camera!"

Flash powder exploded. Puffs of smoke lifted. Those in the rear of the crowd bobbed up and down; waving pads and pencils, striving to capture Bert's attention. Up shot his hands in a plea for attention. Out of his pocket came the Dragon's Eye. He held it up. He turned a complete circle in dramatic fashion; he stood on an upended wastebasket. Whistling, applause, huzzahs, and a barrage of questions from all sides.

"Quiet down, please. I can only answer one question at a time. Which I'll be happy to do to the best o' my ability. Though maybe I oughta just run you all through the whole fascinatin' story, which'll prob'ly answer most o' your questions. An' if you got any more, feel free to butt in an' ask."

He started with the holdup. Ben sighed to himself. It promised to be a long morning. As he listened he sank into a state of stunned amazement. The tale entering his ears bore little if any resemblance to the facts. Bert kept a straight face; his eye was unwavering; he exuded modesty and humility in equal proportions. He described incidents and events, disasters, dangers, and near brushes with death that would have reddened with shame the cheeks of a nickel novelist. He got to the shootout in Reno. " 'Gainst ten to one odds." The two-day chase to Gypsum magically stretched to five days. Interrupted by brief clashes with roving bands of Wichitas and Pawnees, a wild mustang stampede in the dead of night, a prairie fire . . .

The ruby never found its way into his flesh. His appendix incision, which he openly displayed to his awestricken listeners, became a near-fatal knife wound. Incurred in hand-to-hand combat with a Crow subchief. Confrontations and shootouts were commonplace. The train wreck emerged as the worst in the history of U.S. railroading. He personally saved six lives in said catastrophe. He wound up diving, wound and all, into the icy waters of a raging mountain stream twenty times before he found the body of one of the thieves. And recovered the elusive ruby. On and on and on he rolled; he barely stopped for breath; he appalled his son; he bewildered Hume; he enraged Lloyd Tevis. President and chief stood at the railing above listening. While Bert's electrified audience scribbled and snapped.

"Hero's Modesty Matches His Courage," wrote *The Chronicle's* man.

"Father and Son Team Capture City's Heart," wrote *The Bulletin's* man.

"Der Mann von den Stunde Sprict," wrote the *California Demokrat's* man.

Highbinders, hatchetmen, hand-to-hand hostilities, homicides and hair-breadth escapes in abundance. Death defied. Evil overcome. Scoundrels thwarted. Justice triumphing. All in the line of duty.

"What about the ten thousand reward?" asked a reporter.

A bored expression seized Bert's features. He dismissed the money as he might a passing bit of milkweed fluff.

"Duty is its own ree-ward, friend. If they force the money on us, I pledge here an' now before all you witnesses to give my half to the Widders an' Orphans Fund in the name of Wells Fargo."

"Hero's Generosity Marches His Modesty," wrote *The Chronicle's* man.

"Slaughter Rejects Reward for Deed," wrote *The Morning Call's* man.

"Widows and Orphans to Benefit from Hero's Largess," wrote *The Daily Alta California's* man.

Lloyd Tevis had heard all he cared to. He turned from the balcony; he started back up the hallway. His shoulders slumped; his feet dragged slightly. Hume followed him. Tevis's secretary was waiting in his office doorway. She held up a telegram.

"From Washington, sir, the White House. A reply to your telegram."

Tevis frowned. "What telegram? I didn't send any telegram to Washington." He tore open the envelope.

THE PRESIDENT HAS ASKED ME TO CONVEY HIS HEARTIEST CONGRATULATIONS AND SINCEREST BEST WISHES TO YOUR BRAVE MEN STOP NATION DEEPLY INDEBTED TO BOTH AND TO WELLS FARGO

KINDEST PERSONAL REGARDS

A. E. HARTUNG
AMBASSADOR TO BELGIUM

Trevis crumpled the yellow paper into a tight ball. And dropped it at his feet.

"I sent no telegram to Washington," he repeated.

Inside the office Hume closed the door. Tevis went to the wide-open window. He raised one foot onto the sill. He capped his palms over his knee and stared out. For a moment, Hume imagined he was flirting with the temptation to jump. Instead he stared down at the blue-gray water and kept silent. Mute warning to Hume to do the same. He finally lowered his leg and turned to face him.

"I've been thinking." His voice cracked slightly, as if his words were being forced through solid rock. "Maybe we're being a trifle hasty. After all, they did get it back."

"True . . ."

"It wouldn't look good for the company to cashier the town heroes, would it?"

"We'd look like towering ingrates. The press would steamroller us."

"Mmmmm."

Again, prolonged silence. Tevis chewed his lower lip. He shuffled his feet; he sighed heartrendingly; threw his head back awkwardly; assailed the ceiling with a fierce glare. He clasped his hands behind him. So tightly the knuckles whitened. He drilled the rug with his eyes.

"Sometimes I wish I never left Kentucky. Life was so simple back there. No headaches. No ulcers. He'll want a raise. He'll strike while the iron's hot . . ."

"We can't raise him without raising Benjamin."

Tevis shook his head. "It's a bad precedent. From now on everybody who cracks a case will come running with his hand out."

"This case is one of a kind."

"Mmmmm. Two hundred a year seems generous."

"The reward was ten thousand."

"Mmmmm. Well, you work it out. Just don't give them the whole store."

"No, sir."

"What's the time?"

"About nine-thirty."

"Mmmmm." Another heart-rending sigh. "I think I'll go home. Take the rest of the day off. I haven't been feeling all that chipper lately. You and Valentine hold the fort, okay?"

"Yes, sir."

Tevis's secretary stuck her head in. "The Slaughters, sir."

He turned his back on her. In sauntered Bert. Ben followed, subdued looking, self-conscious, still embarrassed by his father's performance.

"Mornin', gentlemen. 'Pologize for us bein' late. Got held up down in the lobby. I swear, I dunno how these newspaper fellas get wind o' things. But they always seem to. Well, here she is, Chief, Mr. Tevis sir . . ."

He held the ruby up and turned it. It caught sunlight and sent it flashing back from various facets. Tevis gave it one look and groaned like a torture victim. A pitiful, soul-wrenching moan. He threw up his hands and stalked out. Bert looked confused after him.

"Did I say somethin'?"

• • • •

Three days later, father and son sat in a bar in little Sausalito. Raking over the coals of the fire of publicity ignited by Bert's lobby speech. Between sips of Haggerty's Morning Dew he browsed through the day's edition of *The Daily Alta California*.

"Offering your half of the reward to the Widows and Orphans Fund was the last straw. Of all the malarky. You know as well as I we're forbidden to accept rewards in cases we're assigned to."

"I know that, you know that, but the reporters don't."

"And what about Doctor Abramowitz? We're leaving him high and dry."

"You mean us promisin' to back up his tellin' how he dug the ruby outta' me? So's he could write it up for the, the . . ."

"*The Journal of Medicine*. That's right."

"What are you, dimwitted? We're sittin' on top o' the worl'. Baskin' in the glow o' all this attention an' esteem. Heroes o' the hour; the company givin' us fat raises. Maybe a bonus even. Presiden' Grant sendin' his own personal congratulations. You wanna kick the props out from under all that?"

Ben sighed wearily.

"You see, you think about it an' you see how foolish it'd be. Don' worry, the doc knows he can't say a word without us backin' him up. I hope he doesn' hold his breath waitin' for me to come 'round."

"What about Captain Powderly? He's got his net spread over the city. He'll catch you and get even if it's the last thing he does."

"Balderdash. Powderly don' care beans 'bout me. 'Sides, he can take a joke. 'Sides that, listen to this right here in this paper. It says 'Police Captain Earl W. Powderly promoted to chief inspector.' For roundin' up all those Sin Yaps, you betcha . . .''

"See Yups. The See Yup tong."

Bert slapped the paper and beamed. "He come up smellin' like a rose, an' we helped."

"*We* did? Enlighten me. Let's see you stretch this one without snapping it in your face . . ."

"We helped by bein' in that den o' infamy. He come to recapture me after they'd busted me outta' his jail. Oh sure, to collar them at the same time. Two birds with one stone. If I wasn't there he wouldn' come. To get all this glory and promotion. Hey, here's somethin' else. 'A spokesman for Wells Fargo announced today that Lloyd Tevis, president and chief operating officer of the company, is taking an extended vacation. Upon the advice of his physician, Mr. Tevis . . .''

"Please, I don't want to hear."

"It's right here in black an' white. Right 'longside 'King Leopol' o' Belgium congratulates brave heroes.' '' Ben got up. He started for the door. '' 'His Majesty extends invitation to father an' son team to visit Antwerp as his honored guests.' Hey, you hear that? Hey, where you goin'? Ben . . . Wanna go to Belgium? He'll give us the keys to the country. Maybe a medal. Hey . . .''

Ben was out of sight and hearing. He walked slowly toward the livery stable. The "joke" played on Captain Powderly he couldn't care less about. But Abramowitz bothered him. He *had* promised him a note backing up the true story.

But if it ever appeared in *The Journal of Medicine* or anywhere else, it would destroy Bert. Abramowitz could see that. Maybe he'd better just drop him a thank-you note. Out of courtesy. He'd read between the lines and continue to keep silent.

He groaned softly. If he really was a hero he felt nothing like one. He wasn't bursting his buttons. Wasn't aglow with pride; wasn't conscious of any great, soul-stirring satisfaction in his breast; wasn't at all flattered by all the attention.

What he was was tired. And still somewhat embarrassed by the three-ring-circus hoopla attending the thing. While Bert was positively reveling in it.

Whoever said like father like son had it all wrong.